INSIDE OUT

The Aftermath

A novel by

Lati`a D. Johnson

Johnson Publications

www.JohnsonPublications.biz

This book is a work of fiction. Names, characters, places and incidents either are products of the author's imagination or are used fictitiously. Any resemblance to actual events or locales or persons, living or deceased, is entirely coincidental.

ISBN 9780615576435

Published by: Johnson Publications

Newtown Square PA

Cover layout/design by Designs by SheShe

Editors: John Andrulis, Victoria Ipri

Printed in the United States of America

Contact for comments or to order books:

www.johnsonpublications.biz

Dedications

To my soul mate, Thank you for looking into my soul and deciding here is where you belong. Your love and energy helps me soar like a beautiful butterfly…
I LOVE YOU.

Thank You

I thank GOD for giving me the ability to express myself freely.

When I say thank you I mean it from my heart to those who love me and those who appreciate my craft. Without my readers I would have no reason to write. I love you all for your support.

My two loving sons you are the reason I strive to reach the stars, so that even if I miss them I will have made them a little closer in your view. You both are my lifeline, thank you for showing me life at its best.

To my daughter thank you for accepting all the love I have to give and returning it a million times over. Many people don't get to choose whom they call Mom. I am proud that you chose me! Keep striving and you too can live your dreams!

To my mother - Thank You for always believing in me and loving me just for who I am; you make greatness look easy.

To my brother and sister: I love you both. I would write a million books to continue to see the proud look in your eyes at the mention of my name.

Thank you to all of my other family and friends, like a circle of light your love keeps me warm in this cold world!

REFLECTIONS

Previously in *INSIDE OUT*

Chapter 14

♫"Don't stop, get it get it! Let me see you pop that pussy DO- DO brown!" TE` pulled up to his coke house to make his weekly visit. He had got his crazy cousin Noah to run his house in the Southwest side of the city. TE` saw nothing but cars and heard loud music blazing from the house.

"What the fuck is going on?" he thought to himself. He felt like he was stuck in a 1993 house party. As he entered the house he could do nothing but smell and see sweaty pussy for miles. He looked around and saw niggas with money everywhere. Bitches were eating each other in the middle of the floor as guys threw money at them. All around the room, niggas were getting lap dances and blowjobs, whichever one they preferred. Noah was nowhere to be seen. When TE` stepped further into the house, he was greeted by a shapely tall Amazon with buttermilk skin. She cornered TE` and bent all the way over, exposing her big, perfectly rounded ass and her pink pussy lips hanging. TE's mouth hit the floor. Big ass was his weakness and had gotten him in trouble many times in the past. Butta lead him to a quiet corner and gave him the VIP lap dance. Five shots later and 30 minutes of dry humping, and TE` was done and on his search for Noah. Noah appeared out of nowhere.

"What's up, nigga?" Noah yelled.

TE` said in a slurred speech, "What the hell is up with this shit? You didn't get authorization for this shit."

"Well, I was meaning to call you; but shit happened so quickly. These little niggas worked hard for a couple of days straight and I figured they could use a little time away from the grind."

TE` straightened his back up. "Look nigga, I deci…"

"Hold up TE`. Let me finish before you go to the moon. We cleared 50,000 in two days with this house alone!"

TE's eyes became wide. He still wanted to check Noah for not consulting with him, but he couldn't ignore the news.

"Damn, Manny and them must not be doing anything this week." TE' was surprised to hear that this one house had exceeded his expectations. He planned on doing 50,000 per week since they were the new kids on the block. This was definitely good news. In the past, all TE` wanted was money, bitches and power. Evea had changed that; he was a family man now. He had too much to lose now. TE` was torn between both worlds. The hunger in his stomach was like a raging angry sea. He was getting completely pulled back into the game and he only meant to wet his feet.

Adam had not called E in a couple of days, since their last encounter. This was not like him not to talk to his sunshine on a daily basis. Evea was up doing some house cleaning. It was early Saturday afternoon when she heard her cell phone continue to ring. She never stopped cleaning because it was an unfamiliar ring tone. Later that afternoon, she checked her messages and realized that Adam had called her from an unfamiliar phone number.

His message said, "Sunshine, it's your baby. Look, I left my program and I'm not going back. I will be at one of my homey's cribs for a few until I can hustle some money up and re-connect with my peoples. I will keep in touch. I love you."

Evea sat there stunned. She could not believe that Adam was now on the run. Evea thought to herself, "How will he survive and where does that leave us?"

Adam made his necessary connections and before one week passed he was back in business. Not to mention his people looked out for him when he hit the bricks. Evea and Adam were definitely a couple. They would go out to fancy places to eat and stay in the best hotels money could buy. Evea was living a double life. She was juggling two men and a home at the same time. Adam became more and more possessive with her. He would start arguments when she would have to go home. The stress of her secret life was killing her. She would cry herself to sleep, at times not knowing which way to go. Adam gave her thug-out love and held nothing back and she liked that. TE` gave her stability and comfort with a sincere love. She was caught in a whirlwind and loving the turbulence. Evea tried to rationalize her indiscretions as she thought to herself, "Shit, men do this shit all the time. They're just not as good at it."

Beee…eep! Evea heard a horn coming from behind her as she pulled out of the parking lot of her job.

"Who the hell is this all up on my bumper?" In her rear view mirror she could see a champagne colored car with deep tint and rims that reflected the sunrays. She stopped to let the idiot go by and realized that it was Adam in his new 2006 Lexus Coupe. He pulled beside her and rolled down the window.

"Going my way, sexy?" he said as he winked at her.

"Whe….n did you get this?"

"This baby is fresh off the showroom floor. Want to go for a spin?"

"Sure, let me park my Jeep."

Evea got in the coupe and her ass melted in the soft supple cream leather seat.

She said, "This shit is hot!"

Adam took off down the highway.

"Where are we going? I have to be home by"…

"SHHHHH, I got you! I want to show you something." Adam took Evea for a long drive to upstate Pennsylvania. The air was crisp and cold as they pulled up to a huge house with horses and other livestock.

"Whose house is this?"

"I don't know but I'm hoping to have one like it real soon. You gone be my part- time wife, taking care of shit." Evea smiled. As silly as it seemed, she liked that idea, even if it was just a dream.

Adam and Evea spent at least three hours more together. When they were together, the time seemed to evaporate like steam from a boiling pot of water. Evea lay gently in his arms gazing up at the sky, wondering how she would continue to pull that shit off.

Adam interrupted her from her trance; "What's up Sunshine? Why you so quiet?"

"I'm just thinking." Evea responded.

"About what?"

Evea thought to herself, "Should I tell the truth or spin it like I know how to do so well?"

I'm thinking about how good it feels lying in your lap and how great it would feel to be riding that big dick right now."

Adam laughed and licked his lips. Evea knew what excited him. He was a true thug, but he liked to be dominated sometimes. Evea could feel his dick rising to its full potential as it throbbed and pressed against the left side of her head. This turned Evea on. She loved dick and loving Adam's dick is just what she proceeded to do. Evea slowly unzipped his Enyce jeans with her teeth. Adams eyes grew with excitement as she used her mouth as a tool. His pants and underwear were pulled down with no hands in the equation. Evea slowly licked around the head of his strong pleasure rod. Her soft full lips melted down the sides of his shaft like warm churned butter, up, around down to the base and back up until she gagged. She went on as Adam's eyes rolled in the back of his head. Evea's deep throat went to the rhythmic sound of his moans. Evea was dripping wet. Her Seven jeans had a huge puddle that started from the front of her crotch all the way to midway her ass. The more Adam moaned, the deeper Evea went until he became close to climax. Evea then slipped a condom from under her tongue and rolled it down his dick as she held the base of the shaft tight to slow the climax down. Adam could not wait to submerge deep into Evea's love pocket. He faced Evea toward the back window of the car, her fingers melted into the butter soft leather as she prepared to be penetrated deeper and deeper. Adam entered her sea with slow and hard pumps. Evea's body trembled from the first stroke. Swap! Swap! Echoed off the windows as he smacked her ass with each stroke. Evea was at her peak with just a few hits.

She yelled, "This shit is great!!!!!!! I'm about to cum! Hit that spot with that big dick!" Screams filled the car with the sweet smell of love in the air. Evea's thick creamy love juice trickled down Adam's pole from top to bottom. They were paralyzed in the moment, until Evea looked at her watch and realized she had to get home before TE` came from picking up Kayla.

"Oh shit, Adam, I got to get back before I'm put on a milk carton."

Evea took out her cell phone to call and check in. She had five missed calls and one text message.

The ride back to the city was quiet. They both hated that they had to depart from one another. Adam rolled down the windows and let the cold crisp air hit him in the face. He was definitely tired after that good shit. He turned his system up and blazed

50 cent's Get Rich or Die Trying all the way in. Evea made it to her truck just in time. She got out and kissed him good-bye. They both did not notice the shiny, new looking black car that obviously had been following them. The tint was too deep to see inside. Adam sat there a little longer just to gather his

thoughts. Even though Adam had money again, status and the love of his life, he felt lonely at times when he just had his thoughts to keep him company. Adam was a tortured soul. He was all alone in his deepest thoughts and he continued to have nightmares of the shooting. Adam was fucked up every since his Father died in the early nineties. He was really close to his Dad and took it hard when he passed on. He felt that he did not have anyone to rely on. His mother was alive, but he felt obligated to take care of her. Adam wasn't always the only child. His brother who was one year younger than him died as a child from a rare genetic disease at the age of three. He had no immediate siblings. He had a long lost stepsister that he never saw who was as fucked up as he was. Adam came up out of his daydream and pulled off. He was headed to meet a realtor about a downtown Condo he was going to rent for a few months until he found a house outside of the city. As he pulled off, he noticed the black car pull off behind him. He slowed down and made a few turns. The car followed him. Adam began to get concerned. He did not know anyone in this car. As he parked again on a busy street, he reached under his seat for his; 38 special. Just then the car passed him and disappeared into the night.

“Maybe I wasn’t being followed,” he thought to himself. He waited about fifteen minutes, then pulled off.

Chapter 15

TE` stumbled from the coke house, barely making it to his car. He called Evea several times and got her answering service. He was in no condition to pick up Kayla. TE` began to get worried. Evea never let her phone stay off this long before. He called his mother in-law and asked could Kayla stay the night because he was tied up at work. His mother-in law said it was okay. TE` watched more niggas arrive at the house as he was leaving. He was fresh out of product and needed to call Lex and order a couple more bricks since this shit moving so quickly. TE` sat in his Escalade with the music loud. He decided to call and put Lex on alert. A Geo Prizm rode around the corner and slowed down as the car approached the house. TE' didn't pay it any mind. He figured it was some more horny niggas coming to the party. Either way the house was cool. It was enough heat in there to start a four-alarm fire. He hit Lex on his phone.

"What up, son?"

"Yo, nigga," TE' responded. "I may need to see you in a couple of days."

Lex responded with, "I'm in the city now on business if you need to talk."

"Nah, not tonight. I'm fucked up. How long are you going to be in Philly?"

"A couple of days. Why?"

"I'll meet you tomorrow at the spot around noon."

"All right One!"

They hung up.

TE` sat there and wondered what business Lex had in the city and why didn't Corn or he know he was in Philly?

TE` looked up and saw that same car coming back around the corner. This time they slowed up at his car. He noticed the passenger was leaning out of the window with burner in hand and began dumping at TE's truck.

"OH SHIT!" TE said as he dove on the floor to get his Glock- 9. He came up dumping back. TE` hit one of them in the shoulder. The party heard the commotion and several niggas on TE`s squad came out blazing. The Prizim sped off with wheels squealing. Noah ran over to the car to make sure that TE` was cool. TE` was untouched but his back window was shot out. All he could think about was what he would tell Evea. Noah told TE` not to worry. He would find out who those niggas were. Noah loaned TE` his Navigator for the night so he would not have to tell Evea the truth.

"If Evea asks, just tell her I'm taking your truck to my homey to upgrade your stereo system. Go home, family man. I'll holla at you tomorrow after I do some investigating."

TE` took the bag full of money out of his truck and gave Noah a couple stacks to get his truck fixed. They said "One" as they embraced and then TE` drove off headed home.

Adam was with the realtor. He gave her the okay to take the condo off the market. He gave her his black card and instructed her to put five months' ~~of~~ rent on the card.

His chirp was blowing up. Adam stepped in the hall to take the call when he noticed it was from Manny's phone. He answered, "Yo, I'm in a business meeting. This shit better be important."

"Adam, meet us at the spot. We were just in a shoot out with theses niggas up the block. Manny was hit."

"Is he hit bad?"

"He was hit in his shoulder. He needs medical attention."

"Alright, take him to the hospital; but remember the rules, snitches get stitches and put in ditches. So Thug this shit out, leave it on the street!"

"All right, later!" Adam returned to his business. Adam apologized for taking so long on the phone.

"That was an important call, sorry."

"No problem, Mr. Artez. I just need one more signature and I can return your license and the keys are yours."

In Adam's business, having several aliases is what got him all that he possessed and protected his real identity.

Ring, ring, ring!

"Hello!" Evea said with an attitude. She did not recognize the number and she thought it was TE` calling her with a story about why he was not home with Kayla yet.

"Hey Sunshine."

"Adam?"

"Yeah !"

"Where you at?"

"In our new Condo downtown overlooking the water I had to call you first with the good news. That was the business I had to take care of tonight. I'm sorry," Adam said. "I'm steady talking. Can you talk right now?"

"Yeah, his ass is not home yet!"

"You sound upset. We're both not having a good night. My young- bull got shot tonight."

"Oh shit! Is he okay?"

Just as Adam began to speak, "Yea….h", TE` was placing his key in the front door.

"I have to go Adam. I got company!"

"I hate this shit!" Adam replied as he hung up the phone.

TE` stumbled in the door.

"Where the hell have you been? Smelling like pussy! And where is Kayla?"

"Kayla is with her grandmother and I don't smell like pussy!"

"I think I know what pussy smells like! I have one."

"Look, I went out wit the fellas for a drink or two and……"

Evea looked out of the back window as she asked, "Who drove….. you….. Where is your truck?"

TE` responded in a slurred speech pattern while he looked in the refrigerator for something to eat.

"Noah got it. I'm getting my stereo upgraded."

"Hold up! You let crazy ass Noah hold your prize possession? Some shit is going on and I'm going to find out what it is!"

TE` straightened up long enough to say, "Speaking of shit going on, why didn't you answer your phone for a couple of hours? That's not like you."

"I…I… my phone was dead. Don't turn this shit on me!"

TE` looked Evea directly in the eyes and said, "Evea Jordan, don't get nobody FUCKED UP! Including yourself. That pussy is mine and all mine. I will go the fuck to jail...."

Evea interrupted with, "Stop talking stupid. That Henney got you fucked up!"

TE` got closer to Evea and began to lick her neck. Evea knew where they were headed. She thought to herself, "Why me? This nigga with Henney up in him can go all night."

She pulled him closer, gritted her teeth and got ready for the ride!

It was early in the morning. Evea awoke to the sound of rain on her window. Her body ached like a tooth that needed to be extracted. Her thighs, legs, ass and especially the kitty cat were thumping. She didn't know she could cum that much in one day. She could smell the rain seeping through her cracked window. The cold crisp air had her nipples at attention. They were even sore. She rolled over to kiss TE` good morning and he was gone. She tried to get her eyes in focus to see the clock. it read 9:22 am. TE` never got up that early when Evea didn't have work. Evea was really suspicious now, but didn't have time for investigation. She had an agenda of her own. She was getting ready to go meet Adam for brunch.

She thought to herself, "Now I don't have to make an excuse to leave the house."

Evea was reluctant to roll out of bed. She needed some more rest. Her bed was covered with her favorite white, soft, goose down comforter that she loved to wrap up in. Evea slowly picked up the phone and attempted to dial the numbers without changing her position. "Shit! I got to get up!" She sat up and dialed the numbers.

"Hello!" A voice yelled.

"Mom, why are you so loud this morning?"

"Girl, what do you want?"

Evea replied, "I want to speak with Kayla."

"What time are you going to get here to pick her up?"

"Probably around 4 o'clock."

"Ok, hold on."

"Hello?"

"Hey baby, are you okay?"

"Yes, I'm having fun with Grandma."

"Mommy loves you a lot I'll be there to get you later."

"OK. Mommy, I love you too, be careful."

Evea hung up the phone and began to get ready for her mid morning brunch with her lover.

TE` was up and out early. He called a meeting at the spot for all of his crew. He planned on meeting about this street business for an hour or so and having everything clear for his meeting with Lex at noon. He sat in a row house in West Philly with heavy security in the area. He was waiting for Noah to get there to discuss business before the actual meeting began. It was enough heat in the house to take out a small country. TE` was in full thug mode. This was war. Noah rode up with music blasting. Biggie's Ready to Die blasted through the streets as he pulled up. He had gotten the window fixed and the truck fully detailed. He entered the house and greeted all that were present. Noah had his pulse on the streets so TE` knew that if anybody knew what was going on it was him. He found out that the hit was ordered by Manny due to his decline in sales. It was supposed to be a warning for the house to close down. They didn't anticipate shooting at the head nigga in charge. Noah was prepared to handle this shit gorilla style. TE` gave him the okay. Noah knew where he hung out and about how many niggas he would have to take out to get to him. TE` explained that he wanted it to be clean and done on neutral territory. Noah understood; that meant no police. The rule they lived by was don't bring heat to your crew under no circumstances. All of the squad was updated. It was almost 11:30 am and TE` had to clear shop before his meeting with Lex.

Lex was funny about people blending in when he was conducting business transactions. He had no friends. He felt they could get too close to his business. His philosophy was friends turn up on the witness stand for the prosecution, turning state's evidence.

He always said, "Travel light, travel far, roll deep and end up behind bars."

TE` played Madden 2006 on PS2 while he waited for the call from Lex.

Evea was dressed to impress and on her way to meet her man. She wore dirty washed denim that sat directly on her hips, a crisp white ruffled shirt and chocolate brown Manolo Blanic stiletto boots with matching purse. Her hair was twisted up in a barrette as her bangs swept over her left eye. She wore very little MAC makeup and natural lip-gloss. Evea arrived at the apartment just a little earlier than planned. She didn't want to go in for long, thinking that Adam would want to finish their business from the day before. She couldn't take any more dicks or tricks. She called Adam and told him she was outside. He told her to come up to see the place. She convinced him that she would come up after they went out. She parked her jeep in the parking lot and stood in front of the door of the building waiting for him. He arrived, looking good as usual.

"Damn baby! I thought I shopped a lot," Evea said when she saw Adam step out of the door in an all blue denim True Religion outfit.

"Every time I see you, you got something new on. Where is your car?"

"The valet is pulling it up."

As fast as he said that, his car pulled up shining like it was off the showroom floor. Evea got in and the valet opened the door for Adam as well.

"Damn! I forgot something, baby. I got to run upstairs."

Adam handed the valet a twenty. The valet attendant closed the car's driver's side door and Adam went back in the building. He had left a bag full of credit cards that he had to deliver in his travels and pick up some money from some clients for.

Just as the car door closed, the same black car that he thought was following him appeared across the street. The driver watched as Adam's car sat there with the engine running.

♫ "I'm conceited, I got a reason…..!" rang from Evea's phone.

"Hello?"

"Hey girl, where are you?"

"Tiff?"

"Who the hell else is calling your ass before twelve in the morning when you should be asleep?"

"I'm sitting here waiting for Adam's slow ass."

"Where?"

"Downtown Society Hill. He got a penthouse condo for us last night."

"Well I'm supposed to meet Lex in a little while for lunch and an afternoon of shopping. After I put this bomb ass on him he can't get enough. I didn't even know he was coming to town. What a wonderful surprise!"

"Don't you mean once you put your freak show together…." Evea replied.

"Bitch, don't hate. You the only one trying to marry a side….."

Beep... Beep... "Hold on. That is my other line." Tiff answered her call waiting.

"Hello!"

"What's up Ma? I'm going to be a little late. I got a little bit of business to handle. I'll get wit you around 1:30."

Tiff said, "It's only 11:50 now. What you got to do?"

"I got a business meeting. See you later."

The phone went dead and Tiff clicked back over to Evea, "Yeah, that was Lex. He's going to be late."

Evea looked up at the large plush building as if she could see inside. "Damn, Adam is taking long! I forgot he had to go to the top floor."

As Evea and Tiff continued to talk, Evea didn't even notice that a black car had ridden up beside the car on the driver's side. She turned around and saw a window rolling down slowly, The next thing she saw was fire from the 45mm sticking out of the window BANG, BANG, BANG, BANG! Evea's voice got weak in mid sentence. Screams rang out throughout the streets. "Evea! Evea! Evea!" Tiff yelled but there was no response. Just as the car was speeding off, Adam emerged from the building, walking and smiling until he noticed that glass was everywhere and people were running and yelling. He ran to the passenger side of his car. There Evea lay. Her body was lifeless, her white shirt was stained with blood and her cell phone was still in her right hand. Adam yelled her name to the top of his lungs but no response was given. He quickly took the phone out of her hand and dialed 911. The ambulance arrived quickly. Tiff arrived at the scene half-dressed and hysterical. She fainted when she approached the car and saw the ambulance and the paramedics trying to get a pulse. They placed Evea's lifeless body in the back of the ambulance and continued to work on her as they blazed through the streets of Philadelphia with the sirens blaring. Adam rode in the ambulance with Evea. He cried and held her hand the entire time. He felt bad knowing that those bullets were meant for him. A second ambulance was called for Tiff. She was on the way to the same hospital being treated for shock.

They arrived at the University of Pennsylvania hospital located in downtown Philadelphia. As they transported Evea's body into the hospital, Adam got out of the ambulance, his tears frozen on his face. He stood outside, scared that if he went in the hospital she would surely die. This is where his father died a sudden death, never to return home several years earlier.

Evea was taken straight to surgery. Tiff was a nervous wreck. She had so many questions. Tiff and Adam's first encounter was inevitable.

"Damn, where the hell is Lex?"

TE`thought as he scored on the game. He looked down at his phone and noticed he had two missed calls and two messages. He didn't hear his phone over the loud surround sound attached to the sixty-two inch TV. He hit his code and noticed that Tiff called him and Lex hit him up. He checked Lex message first, thinking business before pleasure.

"Yo, son, I had to take care of something. I'm running late. I'm on my way, ONE."

TE` finished his game and decided to check Tiff's message.

"TE`, something happened to E. I don't know yet. I'm on my way to her now. Meet us at the hospital. Oh University of PENN."

TE` sat straight up in the chair. His mind wondered, "What could be wrong with Evea? I just left her asleep in bed. And why is she going to the hospital in the city?"

TE` jumped up and sped off without letting anyone know where he was going. TE` could not think straight as he was driving. He was going crazy not knowing what the hell was wrong. The message was left two hours ago and he was in fear of what could have happened in all that time.

Tiff was released from hospital care shortly after being checked out by the doctor. She was eager to lay eyes on the nigga that got her friend in all of the trouble where she may very well lose her life. Tiff scouted the waiting room for Adam. All she had to go on was Evea's description of him. She did not see any fine tall guys looking suspicious in the waiting area. She saw many concerned families waiting for news from the doctor about their love ones. Tiff searched a little more when she remembered that she didn't call Evea's mother. She went outside to use her cell phone. The phone just rang, no answer. When she turned to go back in the hospital, she bumped into a tall caramel color guy with curly black hair.

"Adam?"

"Yes, Tiff?"

"I guess Evea is pretty descriptive, huh?" Tiff commented. Tiff wasted no time to let Adam know their encounter was not a social visit.

"What the hell happened to my friend and why, nigga?" Adam stuttered, "I was in the condo. I don't know."

"You know, muthufucka! They weren't looking for her. She was just sitting in the wrong muthfucka's car!"

"Tiff, it wasn't my fault!"

"Yes the fuck it was. See, I know people like you. Evea's heart is too big and that gets her into shit at times. See me, I would of fucked you and left you where I found you, in the gutter where you belong! But E was manipulated and suckered by a nigga that can't care about nobody but himself!"

Adam became angry and yelled,

"Bitch, you don't even know me!"

Tiff paused and looked at him with a stare that could kill. "I think I do. I've known plenty of niggas like you. Can't live in reality because you don't have a life of your own, so you want to borrow another man's wife and life. If you loved her so much, you would of left her alone when she told you she was happily married."

Adam stood there with a blank look on his face. Tiff had said some shit that he never had been told before. It was as if he was looking in a mirror for the first time.

Tiff continued, "Oh, forgive me if I'm being too blunt and don't buy your "let's do this for the sake of love" speech, but my best friend….. No! correction, SISTER, may be dying in there and I don't see your undying fucking love stopping the bleeding!" Tiff turned around and went back inside of the lobby.

Adam stood there mad as hell and hurt. Tiff just may have hit home.

The doctor swung open the doors leading to the back where surgery takes place. At this very moment, Tiff stood up and greeted the doctor.

"I have bad news," she said, as she stood there in her blood soaked scrubs. At this moment, TE` walked through the door and saw Tiff standing there talking to the surgeon. This scene was in slow motion, like an important scene in a TV drama. She handed Tiff a couple of pieces of paper. TE` approached Tiff as he watched her drop the papers on the floor and break down crying. First, TE` walked fast, then broke into a jog. Right behind TE`, Adam entered the lobby and saw Tiff's reaction. TE` had almost reached her when Adam also took off running. Both men realized they were headed the same way. They both called Tiff's name. Tiff had fallen to her knees while sobbing and yelling, "noooooooo!"

"Tiff, what happened to Evea?" They both said as they reached for the papers at the same time. A look of confusion was fixed on both of their faces, as if to say "Who the hell are you?"

They each picked up a copy of the papers. One was a baby sonogram. Tears streamed down Adam's face like streams of raindrops as they hit a window's glass. TE` stood there in a state of shock.

INSIDE OUT

The Aftermath

A novel by

Lati`a D. Johnson

Chapter 1

Life after love

The cold, hard air entered her lungs, chilling her to the bone. It was strange how quickly it had gotten so cold. The sun was shining on both sides of the street and seemed to be battle the gusts of cold air, leaving portions of the street warmer than others. But there was no doubt about it: old man winter was undefeated.

As far as the eye could see, cars were lined up with bright orange stickers placed in the windshields. People walked up to the front of the church in couples, some crying, others with solemn looks on their faces.

A long, shiny, black stretch Hummer limousine pulled up to the front door. As the door swung open, people stood around and just stared; they wanted to see the family and extend their sympathy. A tall, light-skinned woman emerged from the limo with a look of sorrow. She was dressed in all black and draped in diamonds. She wore a beautiful, long black mink that stretched to the ground as she walked. She looked to be in her mid thirties, but her style gave her age away. Her youthful beauty could be attributed to her pampered living. It was obvious she was the mother of the deceased; people gathered around her and showered her with concerned looks as they hugged her compassionately.

The family entered the church in pairs to view their lost loved one for the final time. A choir sang a comforting hymn. As the song "I Won't Complain" played in the background, people walked up to the casket and placed keepsakes of love in the casket; pictures, money and jewelry were some of the items adorning the deceased. Adam entered the church dressed in all black, wearing a wool suit and a twill jacket.

Adam had not been inside a church since he was a little boy, when his mother would make him go with her to Sunday school. He walked down the center aisle and became overwhelmed with emotion. He was raised in a good home, so the lingering guilt of his thug lifestyle began to weigh on his conscience. Just as Adam looked up to wipe his eyes, a light skinned woman with shoulder-length hair jumped up and let out a scream: "NOOOOOOOOO, NOOOOOO!!!" She wailed as she literally attempted to jump into the casket. Adam watched her and tried to figure out who she was, since she looked so familiar. He looked more closely as he dabbed his eyes, finally realizing that the grief-stricken young women was his long lost stepsister Dashae`, who was also known as Butta.

Adam had not seen Butta since they were children. She got the name Butta due to her golden, silky-smooth skin. She was always in trouble and frequently went against the grain in her youth. Adam thought to himself, "What the fuck is she doing here?" He didn't know why she was there, but he was very happy to see her nonetheless. Memories of their childhood flashed before him- he had so much to tell her. He hadn't spoken to her in years. The last time he saw her was at their father's funeral.

The family comforted Butta and calmed her down as she sipped on a glass of water given to her by the usher. She spotted Adam sitting in the back row with his head down. The funeral went on and the preacher read the eulogy, followed by a sermon. This gave the family hope and comfort during their troubled times. The sermon ended and the preacher called for the last viewing of the body.

The funeral was over and the family headed to the burial ground. Adam stood outside to wait to see Butta. She saw him first.

"Adamie, is that you?" She asked.

"In the flesh baby," Adam replied warmly and playfully. She ran up and gave him a big hug.

"How did you know Manny?" Adam asked.

"Manny and me had a thing going on. That was my baby!" Butta replied, fighting off a wave of emotions. "We didn't let people know about us because of my profession. You know how it is, when niggas know you're somebody's girl… the damn tips get scarce!"

"What type of work you doing?"

"I'm a fucking dancer," Butta said, still grieving, wiping away tears and adding quickly with a smile, "Like you don't know what it is!"

"Manny was my man," Adam said, "This shit is too close for comfort. A nigga tried to run down on me a few weeks ago and some real fucked up shit happened to my girl. Now my fucking nigga gets all banged out. I lost two people in just a matter of weeks!"

"Oh shit, your girl got killed too?" Butta said.

"No, she got fucked up real bad- lost a lot of blood and lost my baby," Adam said without blinking an eye. "To tell you the truth... I don't even know if I still got a girl."

"What's her name?"

"Evea is her name- but I call her Sunshine."

"What the fuck?" Butta said laughing through her tears. "Is she a dancer too?"

"No, I got a professional ghetto queen," Adam said with a wink.

"So, why do you think it is over between y'all?"

"Because her husband kind of gave me that fucking impression!"

"Oh shit!" Butta said; they both started laughing.

"For real though, I fucking love her sooooooo much and she love me." Adam said, almost having to physically shake off the power of the emotions Evea evoked. "It's like we are meant to be together... this shit can't be over."

Butta and Adam left the funeral together. They went to eat at their favorite restaurant and continued their conversation. As they were seated the waitress continued to check Adam out on the sly. She wasn't sure whether they were together or not, so she remained cautious while letting him know she was feeling him. The atmosphere was bright and busy. The waitress made sure she paid close attention to Adam's needs. Butta and Adam would laugh every time she left the table.

Butta joked with Adam as she hit him in the head, "Damn nigga, I don't see why all of these bitches be pressed over your big-head ass!"

They laughed, but then Butta's expression became serious as Adam played with his straw.

"But on some real shit- I missed you."

"I missed your yellow-ass too."

Butta became serious again. "So what do you know about Manny's murder?"

"I got my ear to the street and my finger on the trigger, so don't worry about that shit. Don't nobody come in my house… and shit where I break bread! I got this covered." Adam's eyes were still as ice; he was all business. "I know he was going through it with some new niggas that tried to take over a block down the end. But the head nigga is like a ghost, they don't know who he is." Butta listened intently. "A few weeks ago they lit this nigga up coming out of the new spot, so I think he had something to do with this shit. But since my car and girl got lit-up by some nigga looking for me… I don't know what to think."

Butta replied: "I was working a party a few weeks ago when some shots were fired. But I was in the house working, so I really didn't see what nigga got hit up."

Adam looked Butta in the eyes with a quiet, boardroom seriousness. "Trust what I tell you. This shit is real out here I'm definitely gone peel a nigga's cap about this work!"

Chapter 2

The dead comes alive

Ring, Ring, Ring.

"Hello," a voice cracked on the other end.

"What's up 50 Cent?"

"Tiff?" Evea said in a slightly fatigued voice.

"What's up girl?"

"Get your ass off my phone. It takes you to joke about a serious situation. I can't laugh. My stomach is still sore."

"You're lucky your ass ain't more sore- fucking with TE`'s crazy ass! Speaking of TE`, is he still sleeping in the guest room?"

"Yeah, he don't want to fuck with me, but he wants to make sure I am okay."

"I know TE` ain't trippin' much pussy he done beat up, and you forgave him!"

"Tiff, this shit is different, I was fucking pregnant by Adam- and what's fucked up is I still miss his ass!"

"Bitch, are you high?"

"I'm serious Tiff- this shit is crazy!"

"Bitch, you really are 50 Cent; you done felt how them shells burn and you still won't learn… If you don't- like you know you should- get that no good muthafucka out of yo mind and mouth- it's going to be a 187 for real!" Tiff then said in a concerned voice, "E, can I ask you something? How did you know it wasn't TE`'s baby?"

"Well I know because…" Beep, beep. "Hold on Tiff, that's my other line; as a matter of fact, let me hit you back later. That's a business call."

Evea was happy to be interrupted by the other line, 'cause she knew exactly why the baby she was carrying was Adam's. But Evea felt it was too much info for Tiff to know about her husband: TE` had a life threatening infection a couple of years prior and the antibiotics that he took were so strong that one of the side effects was sterility. TE`s sperm count was too low to reproduce since he was on the antibiotics.

Evea, unbeknownst to TE`, had always wanted more children. She wanted Kayla to have brothers and sisters. It hadn't slipped by her that maybe it was one reason she was so attracted to Adam, the pillar of male virility. He was a lover… and potential father.

When Evea got off the phone with her doctor she laid there in a trance. She could not help but visualize what Adam looked like the last time they met. She curled up in her gray and white cashmere throw and began to daydream about how good it felt just to be with Adam. Evea rested against her goose-feather body pillow as her long eyelashes fluttered with images of Adam. She laid her head on his chest and just listened to his heartbeat. Each breath placed her further into a sweet trance. She could smell his clean-scented cologne, making her breathe deeper a little deeper. She kissed him on his neck as she reached around and caressed his rock-hard abs.

"Damn he feels good!" She said to herself as she kissed him deep and strong, "mmmmm…." She imagined his moaning in a sexy but masculine voice.

"Evea, where are you!" TE` called upstairs, interrupting her sultry dream.

"I'm up here in the bedroom."

Evea was physically shaking as TE` entered their bedroom and broke her out of her daydream. TE`, in a matter-of-fact tone, questioned Evea about her next doctor's appointment. TE` was definitely not happy with their situation. He refused to even look at Evea since that unforgettable night in the hospital.

Evea knew that TE` loved her, but she made no mistake about what made him stay. TE` loved his daughter more than anything: Kayla was a life and marriage saver.

TE` was also a loyal-ass muthafucka. He learned that from being on the street and building his crew from scratch. He knew that a person's word and love for their niggas that held them down was all they had on the street. TE` saw Evea as one of his niggas. She held him down always. And besides that, she was his Baby's Mother (BM) and wife. He also couldn't wait to find the nigga that shot Evea so he could handle shit the right way. One thing TE` could not stand was a sloppy-ass gangster. He was determined to even the score.

Evea lay in the bed trying not to feel really guilty for daydreaming about Adam. TE` was gathering his belongings to get ready to go meet his homeys. Evea questioned TE`, "Where are you going? You just got home…."

TE` continued to take things out of his drawers and didn't even turn around to look at Evea. "I'm going out with Love. We have to discuss some plans for a new job. I'll have someone check on you."

Evea sat there feeling numb. Her heart ached with despair about her once fruitful relationship that was now fucked up, to say the least.

"TE`, why haven't you looked at me since weeks ago?" Evea pushed the issue. She had to get all the tension off her back.

TE` stopped in his tracks as he went to enter the master bathroom. He swung around so fast that he scared the shit out of Evea.

"What the fuck did you just ask me? I cannot bear to look at you! Every time I look at you I see that other muthafucka rubbing and kissing on my body! Damn! Now are you satisfied?"

TE` punched the bedroom door. Evea's eyes opened wide and her breathing sped up as she watched TE`'s anger grow. Evea was happy that Kayla was at her grandmother's house still, so she wouldn't hear them argue.

"I hate this shit!" Te` added in frustration, speaking with his back to Evea. His hands were spread out on each side of the doorframe, Christ-like. Every time I look at you in pain and have to nurse your scars, I'm reminded that this nigga had a piece of you and you almost died for this muthafucka!" Evea sat there with tears streaming down her face. TE` turned around and made eye contact with his wife. He bowed his head in thought, then walked into the bathroom, slamming the door shut. Evea hated what she had done to her life and marriage- but she knew TE` was right. She had let a stranger into their world; now she couldn't shake him from her imagination!

Chapter 3

Lust at first sight

TE` called Love to make sure everyone would be at the spot to discuss business. Love explained that all important parties were informed about the meeting. TE` was dressed to impress as usual, and smelling good. He drove his Tahoe with the music blasting and wheels spinning. He turned heads on every street corner. Classic JAY–Z Fade to Black blasted from his woofers. TE` pulled up to the Pussy Cat and tossed his keys to the valet parking attendant. He stepped out of his truck dressed in a cinnamon brown, pure silk and wool blend blazer, chocolate brown and cream Coogi button-up, dirty-washed True Religion denim pants and matching Kenneth Cole footwear and belt. TE` looked like a million bucks on the outside; but inside, he felt like shit. He was going out with the boys for a meeting mobster style: best bitches, abundant food and stiff drinks.

TE` entered the club and was greeted by a tall, beautiful, deep-dark chocolate colored woman wearing nothing but crystal slippers. The place was full of naked women from every part of the world. The air was filled with the aromatic smell of jasmine and other sweet herbs. The spot wasn't the average booty bar in the hood. This was an upscale gentleman's club for true ballers. The woman led TE` to the VIP section where Love, Jay-Rock, Noah, and Corn sat waiting for him. The boys did not mind the wait; they had plenty of curvaceous entertainment to occupy their time. Noah was loud and crazy as usual. He had two Persian bitches on his lap, rubbing their breasts and smacking their asses. The rest of the crew sat there joking about how Noah didn't know what to do with them hoes. TE` walked up and everybody greeted him.

"What's up my niggas?" TE` responded with a big smile. TE` gestured for the waitress and ordered a bottle of Hennessey and a round of Coronas. The business meeting was on.

"Today was Manny's funeral and our informant said that there was no cops at the funeral. That's good. That mean my man over here handled shit correctly," TE` said as he looked to Noah. "The next problem at hand is getting the house down the end flowing again. I have not heard from Lex since a couple of weeks ago when he left a message on my phone." TE` scanned his homeys, making eye contact with each and every one of them, making sure they were real.

"Corn, you think you could get at him for me?" TE` said, less as a question and more as a designation of the next order of business.

"Yeah, I can holla at him when I order my shit," Corn replied.

"The real issue that got me fucked up right now is this nigga is still on the loose that shot Evea up. Did anybody hear or see anything?"

"Nah, the shit happened far out of the 'hood and nothing hit the streets yet," Noah replied.

"Yo, I don't know why you ain't smoke that pretty muthafucka Adamie or whatever his fucking name is on sight," Jay-rock exclaimed, sick of all the buuulllshiitt. "That pussy is still walking around a free man. That shit ain't cool."

TE` leaned over and spoke in a calm voice, "Look Jay. I know you heated about this situation, but trust me. Mr. Pretty Boy is being used as Bait. When the muthafucka realizes that he missed his mark, he will be back to finish the job- and that is when I'm going to kill two birds with one NINE!" They all laughed and gave each other dap while cracking up.

"Now business is finished. It is time for Pleasure and Sexy and Candi and…." Love crooned.

"We get the picture," they laughed, more at Love's exuberance, than what he said.

TE` signaled the host and before they knew it- VIP was full of pussy. "I'm In Love With a Stripper, She Rocks it She Rolls it ……" The boys sang along as the strippers gave out lap dances on cue. A slow, sexy chime sounded and the dancers stopped like they were placed on pause.

Noah howled in complete disappointment, "What the fuck happened? Why did the ass stop clapping?"

They all turned around and saw that the lights throughout the entire place went dim. The only light in the place was a spotlight on the stage. A sound roared through the sound system: "I Found You Miss New Booty Turn Around Bring It Back To Me, Booty Booty Booty Booty Rocking Everywhere!" A sexy, shapely woman slid down the pole from the ceiling to the floor, spinning around the pole and clapping her ass to the bass line. All eyes in the place were on her.

The flashing lights danced off of her smooth, golden skin, like reflecting diamonds. Her rhythmic movement mesmerized them all. Her body was a slave to the beat. It did exactly what the beat commanded. Her beauty and serpentine motion made dicks rise like North African cobras. As TE` watched her, he thought there was something familiar about the tall refreshing drink: and he was thirsty. Her body was a vision of perfection. She possessed an ass only seen on music videos, perfectly rounded and smooth as freshly spun silk. She spun around and faced her bare ass toward the crowd. As she bent over, exposing her all, she removed her sparkling g-string all in one motion. There she stood, illuminated, fully exposed. The club went wild. TE`'s eyes were riveted. She slithered off of the stage, entertaining the crowd by laying her g-string on an older man's bald head. She walked among her transfixed congregation, setting fires of desire as she brushed pass them. She looked up and spotted TE` staring directly at her. They caught eyes and she proceeded to strut up to him. Before he could say anything, she mounted him like a prized thoroughbred racehorse. Her hips spun and gyrated out of control. She was enjoying the lap dance more than him. She rode him for two more songs until TE` finally- and physically- acknowledged her presence. She burned white-hot, leaving sweet juices all over his pants and TE` in a trance.

The boys continued to enjoy their night out, but TE` could not get the girl out of his mind. The club was about to close and he let all of his homeys ride out. He stuck around hoping to get to talk to the Beauty that had just put cum all over his new jeans. He sat in his truck waiting patiently.

Ring, Ring.

TE` answered his cell phone impatiently, "Yo, what's up?"

A voice echoed through the phone, "Hey sweetheart, where are you?" It was Evea checking up on him. TE` began to speak… but suddenly there she emerged from the club: his long awaited desire, looking as sexy in clothes as she did *au natural.*

TE` paused, then said as if speaking to a child. "E, I will see you when I get home."

The phone went dead in Evea's ear. She sat there staring at the phone, livid, lost in thought, like it was going to ring again from her mental telepathy.

TE` yelled out of the window of his truck, "Excuse me Miss, don't I know you from somewhere?" She kept walking. TE` followed it up with, "Do you always love 'em and leave 'em?" She stopped dead in her tracks and turned around, getting ready to spit hellfire, until she realized that TE` was the nigga that had just made her cum from dry humping (and not to mention she could smell good dick and money from miles away).

"Do you always harass strange single women at 2 am?" She replied with a sexy smile and desirous laugh.

"I didn't know that offering a beautiful young lady a ride home was harassment," TE` said playfully. "And as far as I can remember, we are anything but strangers… you came all over my jeans an hour ago."

"Damn I can't believe you mentioned that," Butta replied. "I'm so embarrassed. That shit has never happened to me before."

TE` stood there liking her even more as they continued flirting, "I knew you looked familiar. Were you a dancer at a house party down the bottom a couple of weeks ago?"

"Yeah" she replied, "I knew you felt familiar," she said with a smile. "You were 'Mr. Hennessey' in the corner."

"Oh shit, I knew you looked too well kept to be working in a house party. What's your name again?" TE` asked with a big smile.

"You can call me Butta."

TE` laughed and said in a slow, deep voice, "Smooth and creamy like butter."

"That's right: soft, smooth and creamy."

TE`'s loins were on fire. All he could do was admire the spectacular view.

Flashing lights reflected off the bedroom windows. The rocks that lay in the driveway cracked under TE`s truck tires. He walked slowly down the driveway path and reminisced about his evening. He placed his key in the door and before he knew it the door swung open.

"What the hell are you still doing up and why are you out of bed?" he yelled.

"No, the question is- where have you been? And why the hell do you have that goofy-ass grin on your face?" Evea knew that look all too well, which was the look of some new pussy in the wing. She might have almost died, but she wasn't going to roll over and play dead. She was hangdog, feeling low over her affair with Adam, but her pride was still well intact.

"Last time I checked I was a grown-ass man! And I don't need another mother!" TE' replied, as he walked passed Evea to the refrigerator.

Evea wasn't going to back down. "Look TE`, I get it! I fucked up tremendously. I can't take back what I did, but I know I love you… and never wanted to leave you or hurt you. I hate this shit. I feel like a stranger in my own home. I can't stand how you look at me with this strange mix of pity and anger in your eyes. Man, I'm still your wife! I'm still a woman! I'm still your lover!" she said, turning her anger to raw emotion.

TE` just stood there, fucked up over the words that were raining out of Evea's mouth.

"Evea, I don't know what you want from me. I can't just pretend like this shit never happened! I know I fucked up in the past. But those hoes knew their place; they were never special. But you… Fuck it. You were sporting this nigga like a Fendi bag!"

Evea cut him off mid sentence with a soft, hot, wet kiss. TE` fought it at first but his dick didn't argue at all. Evea hadn't forgotten how to make TE` melt like a snowball on a summer day. She dropped down straight to her knees and unbuttoned his pants.

Slowly she kissed the head of his dick like it was kissing her back. She could tell TE` wanted more so she consumed his rock-hard missile like a multi-vitamin. She took him straight down her throat. TE` became more and more excited as he watched her take all of him in her mouth. TE` struggled from mixed emotions. He closed his eyes and put his head back and visions of Butta ran through his mind. But he was definitely ready for some pussy. He gently lifted Evea up and placed her on his lap. His dick was so hard that Evea came back to back just from a couple of pelvic thrusts. TE` was hitting that ass from the bottom like he was on top. His pumps got faster and more intense. Evea knew what that meant. She squeezed down and tightened her pussy walls fast then slow, over and over again. "OOOOOOOH shit!" TE` yelled. He shook uncontrollably, sending Evea into a frenzy.

"Give me all that sweet love!" She yelled as she came all over again like the last encore at an Usher concert. They both lay there paralyzed, at peace, without judgment in the moment- and not wanting the feeling to end.

Chapter 4

Needle in a hay stack

The sun was shining brighter than usual this particular day, so Lex thought. He had just come back from a long weekend in Jamaica with Tiff. Tiff had to blow off some steam to get the shit back at home off her mind. Lex rode from the airport in his new toy- his 2006 Danali truck. He thumped 2Pac all the way down the road. The system was so loud he could barely hear his phone ring. "We trade war stories...." the chorus sang. Lex felt his two-way vibrate. It was a message from his Philly connection. He turned the music down and got out his business phone.

"What up Son!"

"My nigga what's up with you?" Corn replied. "I thought you fell off of the face of the planet."

"Nah, nigga I'm still shining," Lex said in his chill way.

"I see. I need some work, you got me?" Corn said straight-up.

"I think I can get you a few interviews lined up. You still in the same line off work?"

"Yeah, about how long you think it will be?" Corn continued. "My homey needs a few gigs lined up in brick laying." "Give me a day. I'll contact you, ONE." Lex hung up the phone and turned up 2Pac.

Tiff just sat there staring at her sexy-ass gangsta. Tiff and Lex were on the way to one of Lex's New York apartments in downtown Manhattan. From there, they were going to the parking garage to pick up Tiff's car. Lex looked away. When he turned around and realized Tiff was still looking at him, he questioned, "What's wrong, sexy? I noticed you have been preoccupied the entire trip."

Tiff was falling hard for Lex. But one thing was for sure. Tiff wasn't sloppy. She did not trust anyone, and definitely not any nigga- no matter how big his dick was. She did not talk about her personal life, like friends and places where her people stayed. She figured that the type of niggas she dealt with was capable of anything, no matter how trustworthy they came across. She did not want to leave room for revenge at her expense, just in case she had to fuck them over. Lex was the same way; he never discussed his business with females. Tiff respected that. They were a match made in heaven… or so they thought. The primal natures of their personalities- as all wild animals- made them dangerous, hunted targets. But , living in the Now is what mattered to them- and they were kickin' it on Cloud Nine.

Tiff turned around, looked at Lex, and said, "I'm cool. This is a small thing- nothing I can't handle."

Lex smiled and replied, "I almost forgot how sexy and tough you are all at once."

"And don't you forget it!" Tiff winked and blew a kiss at Lex, just like the true diva she was.

Lex dropped Tiff off and headed for the 'hood to check on some shit. As he pulled off, the thought of going to Philly crossed his mind. He figured he would holla at his nephews (since they handled the details of his business) to see if they heard anything about their Problem. He dialed Rizz and got no answer. As he was hanging up, his phone rang.

"What up?"

"Yo, L-Raw, what's poppin'?"

"Sin, that you?"

"Yeah nigga, who else calls you L-Raw?

"Damn, where have you been?"

"Around. Yo son, did you hear anything else about The Problem?" Lex asked.

"Nah, I even scoped the news for that shit. That nigga wasn't even important enough to make the eleven o'clock news, that pussy," sneered Rizz.

"Hold up. You heard nothing… then how do we know this problem is solved?" Lex asked, with a hint of concern in his voice.

"Because nobody haven't seen or heard from The Problem in weeks. The ride is even missing, " Rizz said confidently, if not because he fully believed it but at least to alleviate Lex's worries.

"All right Son. I will be in town tomorrow. I'll get at you then, ONE." Lex knew he was a 99 outta 100 shooter, but something did not seem right about that shit. His gut told him something was off.

Adam woke up with the sun shining directly in his eyes. He had moved to a new location where no one knew where he was. He was on the top floor of the building overlooking the Walt Whitman Bridge, which links Philadelphia with Camden. The downtown skyscraper was beautiful in the morning light. He had not put anything up to the windows because he had no nosey neighbors on the 85th floor. Adam changed up his whole routine. He got a new car with tint so deep and dark, he could barely see out. He was now whipping in a platinum 2006 Jaguar, with spinning rims and a charcoal black leather interior. Adam became the leader of the crew Manny had left behind. He was determined to find out who killed his brother-in-arms.

Adam had left the drug game alone for a while, before he got booked in his last case. He now had a lucrative credit card business. But he hated the thought of leaving his niggas out there on the streets after Manny got knocked, so, once again, he became the boss on both fronts. It felt funny to him: holding daily meetings with the little corner hustlers and getting back in touch with all of his old connects. It was not hard, Adam being the one to hand shit to Manny when he got locked up some years ago. His connects respected him and was ready for the business.

Adam got out of bed to get ready for his meeting with his new right-hand man. Well, he was Manny's right-hand man. Adam did not trust him and he wasn't sure why. Zayne was straight gorilla tactics. He did not give two fucks about anybody that got in his way. He was a young-bull, but he was definitely ready.

Zayne walked with a swagger that challenged all niggas. He kept his M-1 on him at all times. He always joked about never getting caught without ammo. His gun was always loaded with 100 bullets for 1 to a 100 niggas- or whoever wanted to test him. Adam was an Alpha male himself and did not like anyone who challenged his prowess. Zayne was six feet tall, with skin smooth as chocolate mousse. His bright white smile was captivating and a favorite among the ladies. His sexy looks and boyish charm could get him in anywhere. This was his best asset: he fooled enemies into believing he was soft and naïve- and then took them out with a smile and a cap. He never parted from his gun even when he slept. His gun was so special he named it, Na Na, after his girl, Naih.

Adam was not exactly excited about their meeting and trying to partner with Zayne.

Chirp, Chirp.

"Yo, you solo?"

Adam looked at his mobile and said to himself, "What the fuck do this nigga want?"

Chirp, Chirp.

"Yo, I'm cool, what's up?" Adam said.

"I'm at the spot. Are you on your way?" Zayne's voice came across loud and clear on Adam's chirp. So loud that he tried to turn down the volume to just get that nigga outta his face.

"Yeah nigga, what? You the Time Keeper now?"

"Nah nigga, I'm the clip spitta and the money geta!" Zayne said as if he was the second coming of Don King.

Adam couldn't resist mocking him, "Oh shit nigga, what you MC-Gangsta now?"

Zayne became impatient with their banter, "Nigga, never mind who I am, just get here so we can get this money!"

Adam gritted his teeth, bit his tongue and proceeded to wait until his car was pulled up. As he stood there in his tan Woolridge and his fresh tan Timberlands, he thought back to that day his world was forever changed. He fell into a trance. All he could see was Evea's bloody shirt. Horns blared and brought him out of his daydream. He blinked his eyes and found his finger on the trigger of his nickel-plated Desert Eagle. He shook it off and got in his car. He wanted more than anything to contact Evea, but he did not know what to say.

Adam pulled up and drove around the block a couple of times to be sure he was alone. The block was a typical city block with about 60 houses on the street. The house he would enter was in the center of the block. The porch was made to look like a family lived there, so they would blend into the neighborhood while conducting business. Adam parked his car in the back driveway.

Adam exited his car, but still did not feel completely safe. He was extra careful to look all around him. He walked, pausing every so often to assure himself that he wasn't being followed. He bumped into several kids on their way to school.

"Sorry little man," he said, looking behind him at the kid who stumbled and whose books fell to the ground. The street was busy with people leaving for work. The air dripped with the smell of bacon and eggs. Adam reflected on how he used to be when he was their age, innocent and trusting- before he was adopted by the streets.

He finally made it to the house and walked up the steep, crooked stairs. Agitated, he knocked impatiently on the door. He could not stand all the damn rules Zayne had. He couldn't go through the back door because Zayne would surely shoot first and ask later. Zayne recognized the knock at the door. He stepped a few feet back with his gun pointed directly at the door. Adam entered.

"What's up wit ya?" Zayne said with a big grin on his face.

"Nothing. I'm ready to take care of business," Adam said as he panned the room behind Zayne.

"Okay Donald Trump!" Zayne joked mocking his business-like demeanor.

The two men sat at a large table in a dimly lit room. They discussed current business and how they were going to take their 'hood back from the new ballers. Adam listened to Zayne talk about how he thought shit should be handled. His methods were of course aggressive and violent: running up in the house and bangin' all who's present type shit. Adam was no joke or candy-ass, but he preferred to use the subtle and calculated approach to fish the niggas out that killed Manny. They agreed to chill on the gorilla warfare shit, sending something a little softer to cushion the blow. Same result, less mess.

Adam explained to Zayne that he was in charge of the daily run of the business. Zayne was only to contact him when it was time to re-up or when there was a serious problem that may compromise their operation. Zayne and Adam discussed possible enemies who may have wanted Manny dead. They both took a handful of profiles off the table and mutually agreed to do some investigating of their own.

Adam left the house with the feeling that their meeting went better than expected. He walked down the street a little more relaxed then he was when he first arrived. He said to himself, "Damn. Time goes fast as shit when you're not paying attention to it." His attention turned to his growling stomach. This reminded him of Evea, because he hated eating alone since they'd met. He was so used to her company that he almost became physically ill without her. He made it to his car safely and sat there for a minute as he gathered his thoughts about the profiles he'd obtained from Zayne. He started to think that maybe Zayne was bonafide young-bull after all (or else a member of the

CIA). Adam appreciated and respected how much Zayne thought things through. Most niggas in his line of work have all the fire and passion, but no smarts. Zayne was different- he had his own way of thinking. Zayne had a habit of breaking situations down and attacking them systematically, one part at a time, so he wouldn't miss anything.

The profiles Zayne provided on their enemies had so much information on each of them: name & alias, close friends, chill spots, all cars driven, bitches in tow, caliber and number of guns carried. The profiles were very useful. So useful that Adam was curious about how and where Zayne got his hands on the information. He remained suspicious.

Zayne sat there and stared at the profiles that remained. In his head, he went over how he would check up on the niggas. In the meantime, he made the moves he needed to set things in motion.

Chirp, Chirp. "Sexy, you free?" Zayne said, leaving his business behind.

"I'm here Ziggy…"

"What I tell you about calling me that shit?" Zayne yelled into his phone.

Naih laughed and replied in her normal tone of voice, "Nigga, what's up?"

"You know what's up. I need you to come through."

"You're at the usual spot right?"

"Yeah, holla at me."

"I'll be there in twenty minutes Ziggy!" Naih laughed as she took her finger of off the chirp button on her Nextel phone. Naihira, "Naih," as she was called for short, was the perfect blend of street and sexy, homey and lover. She and Zayne met years prior, when the two were locked up in juvenile prison. They were attracted to each other instantly. This was surprising, not because Naih wasn't drop-dead beautiful; but she was just not Zayne's usual "high yellow" pick. Naih stood 5'5" and had chestnut brown eyes that lit up a room. She was the classic image of an Egyptian Goddess. Her skin was a deep dark, almost the color of a black sand beach, and smooth as sea glass. Her body was constructed like an Italian sculptor's long-awaited masterpiece. She was thick and juicy like a top sirloin steak. Her ass sat low and was plump and perfectly proportioned with her thighs and hips. Her breasts were substantial and stood straight out without a bra. Her long black hair fell down to the middle of her back. Zayne, like all other men, could not resist her beauty and charm, as if she could cast spells at will. She won men over with her wit and raw street-savvy attitude.

Naih and Zayne were inseparable for years. But they had a harsh dose of reality when she was almost his Baby-Mother. Naih's fast upbringing and all of her trouble with the law left no room for a baby. After Naih got rid of Zayne's baby, he never looked at her the same way again; but they remained friends.

Zayne sat in a single leather chair watching videos on the big screen plasma television. His gun on his lap and pussy on his mind kept him alert while waiting for Naih. Zayne heard two taps and one chirp sound come over the walkie-talkie on his phone. This was their code. Naih was at the door and Zayne could not wait to see her. Zayne approached the door as usual: gun in hand, pointed directly at the door. The door swung open and there she stood in a Charlie's Angles stance, 380 in her hand. Zayne looked her up and down and said, "You one gorgeous gangster." They both laughed.

The door closed behind them and their laughter quickly turned into silent and lustful admiration. Zayne approached her and pushed her up against the wall of the living room. He bit her neck aggressively while unbuttoning her FranKie-B jeans. He licked in long strokes from her neck down her cleavage and sucked both nipples like tender cherries. Her moans filled the air like a sweet love ballad. Naih could not get Zayne's clothes off fast enough. She brushed her hand over his jeans as she was attempting to take them off and discovered exactly what she came for. Zayne picked her up as she rested the top of her back on the wall. Their clothes littered the floor like the Monday morning rush at Goodwill. Naih slid down on his dick as if her body was custom fit and hand molded for it. The sweaty smacks of their skin touching, clapping, echoed throughout the room. She gyrated her hips while he used his hands to palm her ass. They performed like jungle animals for an entire hour until Zayne yelled, "I'm about to cum!" The walls shook. He slumped over on Naih's back like he was shot. Naih rolled over and just stared at the ceiling. They were silent except for their relaxed breathiing.

Naih broke the silence; "So what's going on ?" As much as she enjoyed their 'business' meetings, she knew it came with a price or a favor.

Chapter 5

The Comeback Kid

Evea pulled up to the front door and left her car double parked while she went in to punch the time clock. Upon entering the building, she passed many of her co-workers and they just stared at her as if she was an exhibit at a museum. Evea was not yet adjusted to traveling outside by herself. She reached the time clock, then hurried back to her car to park. Evea felt self-conscious about the circumstances surrounding her injuries.

She was on her way back in the building when she encountered Ms. Cece, who gave her the concerned look and asked her how she was coming along with her recovery. Evea stood there and entertained her questions for a few minutes. Evea thanked Ms. Cece for her concern.

Evea was finally inside of the prison after going through three checkpoints. She was almost to her office when she bumped into Craig.

"Hey Mrs. J, we missed you here. Where were you?" he asked.

Evea looked at Craig and knew from the look on his face that he knew what had happened; at least he knew the story she told the administration. Her mind wandered back to that day. Her breathing sped up. Craig broke the spell with a loud voice, "Mrs. J! Are you there?"

"I'm cool, Craig. I was just daydreaming," Evea said. "Come to my office later and I'll fill you in on the details of my absence."

"I'll holla at you later then." Craig walked away knowing he had just experienced a professional spin move.

Evea arrived at her office. She entered the room and simply stood there looking at her desk. It was exactly as she had left it more than six weeks ago, but Evea felt like she was in a foreign country. Well into the lunch hour, people came by her office to welcome her back. Even people she did not know wished her well and welcomed her back.

Evea was gathering her things and getting ready to go to lunch when the phone rang.

"Mrs. Jordan speaking," she answered.

"What up my nigga? You back like Jay-Z!"

"Tiff get a life!" Evea knew that it could be nobody but Tiff, always saying some fly shit.

"How is my 50 Cent doing today?"

"Fuck you," Evea replied jokingly, before Tiff was even done speaking. "I'm cool though. I just didn't realize it was going to feel this funny coming back to this place."

"What did you think? You were going to float through the doors of the Ritz Carlton Hotel? Of course it feels funny- it's Prison!" Tiff laughed. "The same type of niggas that may have shot you or someone else, surrounds you all day long."

Evea was silent during the pause.

"You will be all right as the days go on." Tiff said, not joking anymore.

"Tiff, you always have to say some smart shit!"

"Yo," Tiff wanted to change the subject. "I called you to tell you about my getaway with Lex. We had a ball. Although I thought about your ass the entire time- you were fucking my flow up. I only fucked four times!"

"What?" Evea questioned. "How long were you gone?"

"Three days. You know I got to get my shit off at least twice a day!" Tiff laughed.

Evea was silent.

"Fifty, don't get mad cause you ain't getting your kitty-cat stroked," Tiff teased.

"Bitch, please!" Evea busted out. "For your information, I was stroked, petted and fed… quite well I may add, a couple of days ago!"

"Oh shit! TE` gave some love stick up! That's what's up! My girl is back. I just know you betta get that other dick out of your mind and…"

"Tiff," Evea cut her off, "I got to go. I'm on my way to lunch."

"Yeah I know you can't stand the heat. I'll holla later."

Evea left for lunch. She walked down the long, sterile hallways to get to the front of the prison. The walls were painted stark white and the floors were a neutral ivory and buffed to a shine. She passed several inmates in the hall. She pondered what Tiff said. As she passed each inmate, she thought, "It could be any one of these mutharfuckas I'm passing that shot me." As she reached the front door she could feel the sweat beading up on her forehead. She was searching her oversized Chloe purse for a napkin when her phone rang. Evea stood there nervous and sweating. But she was still a sight for sore eyes, even in her panic. She wore a tea-length denim skirt with a matching tapered denim blazer. Her soft cashmere sweater gently hugged her soft breasts. When she bent over, her spiral curled hair fell over her right eye. Evea struggled to find her phone before it stopped ringing.

"Hello!" she yelled as the cell phone almost slipped out of her hand.

"Sunshine, are you there?" Evea froze in her tracks as tears streamed down her face. She knew only one person called her Sunshine. Adam caught her off guard and the mixed emotions overwhelmed her.

Lex arrived in town early. Lex liked to do business during the week because there weren't that many drug stops during rush-hour traffic. Corn met him at their usual spot. Corn sat in his newest toy, a pearl colored 2006 Ferrari with butterfly doors and soft smoked gray seats. He arrived a few minutes early to case the area for suspicious activity. Lex drove up in his wide body Denali. They both emerged from their vehicles and greeted each other with a pound.

"What up Son? Long time no see."

"I been kind of busy with some personal shit," Corn replied.

"Yeah, I see you eating well," Lex joked.

Corn kept the conversation to a minimum. Lex was cool, but he was considered suspect due to his disappearing act.

"You got TE`'s shit too?" Corn questioned. "Where is he?"

"TE` don't do early meetings. You know he's a fake-ass working man." They laughed. Lex pointed to a black bag in the back of a car parked on the street. "It's all there." Corn checked the packages and everything was cool.

"I didn't know what to think since I last spoke to TE`," Lex added. "I got to the spot and TE` was

nowhere to be found. Is he cool?"

"Yeah, he had an emergency that day."

"I figured that, because the front door of the spot was left open," Lex said. "I've been going through some minor crew shit myself. In fact, I'm about to meet up with my nephews in a minute to work this shit out. Yo Son. Tell TE` to keep his head up, ONE."

Corn left TE`'s shit in a nearby car and both men went their separate ways.

Chapter 6

New beginnings

The sky was clear and the air was crisp. Evea boarded the plane and sat down in the window seat. She called her mother-in-law to check on Kayla and tell her she loved her. As the plane took off she could see the clouds getting closer and closer. She took a deep breath and closed her eyes. She awoke to the flight attendant directing the passengers as the plane landed.

TE` asked Evea in a soft tone, "Are you up, sleepy head?"

Evea rubbed her eyes to get them in focus. "Yes, I'm trying."

As they departed from the plane, Evea was still groggy. That did not stop her from appreciating the beautiful surroundings. She could smell the fresh tropical flowers permeating the airport. Just outside was a natural waterfall. Fiji was gorgeous. TE` walked a few steps behind Evea, carrying the luggage through the airport. His thoughts were a little different than Evea's. He thought about how different his New Year's would have been if Evea had died in the shooting. Evea saw that TE` was in deep thought.

She looked at him and said, "Baby, I cannot believe this shit. I am so lucky to be here with you. I LOVE YOU!"

As Evea said those words, TE` broke out of his trance and said, "E, the hotel transportation should be here before you know it."

Evea thought to herself, "Damn! That's all he has to say after all of that?"

Evea and TE` made it to their suite. They were in the best hotel in Fiji. Their room's balcony overlooked the ocean and was draped in silks. Precious stones were perfectly placed throughout the suite. The suite came equipped with their own butler to wait on them hand and foot. A handcrafted hammock swung on the balcony next to the stairs that led them to their private pool. Evea was feeling sexy as soon as she entered the bedroom. The bed was huge. It sat four feet off the ground and was encased in four solid gold canopy poles. Fresh flowers were placed all around the bed and a fresh bottle of Cristal champagne sat on ice next to the bed. Evea began to undress. She wanted TE` to see her beautiful, smooth body when he entered the room. Evea was so horny that she began to separate her wet juicy lips and gently rub her soft pink clit. She began to moan with sexy purrs at the end of each grunt. TE` heard the noise as he tipped the busboy at the suite door. He hurried upstairs to discover Evea masturbating, rubbing up and down on eight hundred thread count Egyptian cotton sheets. TE`s manhood was swelling. The arch of Evea's back made TE`s dick rise and jump like Vince Carter dunking the ball. Evea got up on one of the poles at the right corner of the bed and gave TE` his own private show. Their vacation got off to a sultry start.

Back in the states, crowds filled the stores trying to get ready to usher in the New Year. People made resolutions that 2006 would not be better than 2005. Tiff was out at the mall trying to get the perfect New Year's outfit to fuck Lex's head up. Tiff was not like other people. She definitely was not going to spend New Year's Eve with no nigga. At least that is what she told herself to convince herself that she was not falling hard for Lex. She agreed to celebrate at the same club he would be at; not like a date. She called all the girls to make sure they would be ready to descend on the club.

The streets were full. The lines to the club were like in the movies. They wrapped around the block twice. Bitches were outside at nine o'clock on the dot, just to be sure to get into Club Abode. They were half-dressed like it was mid July. They were dressed in short flashy dresses and draped in diamonds. The men were sexy sheik in their velour blazers and button ups, with blingin' cufflinks and high quality denim.

Tiff, Peaches, Plummie, Sassy and Kiwi arrived around eleven o'clock. The line was still long and frozen in time like a still photo. Tiff stepped out of the limousine one leg at a time. Her legs were gorgeous. She wore a fire red, strapless Ferragamo mini with diamond and satin tie-up strappy Manolo Blahnik heels. The rest of the crew followed her lead. Plummie adorned her tall, thick chocolate frame with bronze and cinnamon. She wore a one-piece DKNY halter expressing two of her best assets. Peaches followed up with a silver vintage gown, fully exposing one leg with matching sling-back Kenneth Cole four-inch stilettos. Sassy did not get her nickname by being sweet. She set the crew on fire with her two-piece Ann Klein mink booty short outfit, complete with thigh-high Marc Jacob boots. Kiwi smoothed the crew out with her True-Religion after-five collection. She draped her golden bronzed body with a spaghetti strap one-piece cocktail dress fitted at the waist and breasts, with matching open toe denim stilettos.

As the girls got out of the limo one at a time, heads turned and stared. Tiff walked straight to the front of the line and the bouncer lifted the chain and all the girls entered the club. A soon as they walked in, guys flocked to them as if they had a sign saying FREE PUSSY WITH EACH DRINK PURCHASE on their heads. Tiff headed straight to the VIP section where their table was already set up. She canvassed the club for Lex, but here was no sign of him. The club was on fire with raw energy. Everybody was dressed to impress and getting fucked up. The girls went on the dance floor and got lost in the crowd. Tiff sat back sipping champagne. She felt a tap on her shoulder. She swung around, about to say some smart Tiff-shit, when she realized it was Lex, looking good as gold.

"Are you waiting for someone?" Lex asked suavely.

"No, not really," Tiff said with a devilish grin, adding with a touch of attitude. "Nigga, you just made it before twelve o'clock. You was about to be on the exclusive Tiff Shit List- and that list is easy to get on… but hard to get off." They both laughed. Lex sat down and ordered them a drink. The entire club counted down as the New Year came in.

"HAPPY NEW YEAR!" They all yelled.

For a brief moment the music stopped and nothing but unfamiliar voices filled the air with screams of celebration.

♫"I GOT THE RIGHT TEMPERATURE TO KEEP YOU WARM" sang out over the crowd. Everyone screamed and sang along with Sean Paul. The party raged.

In the back corner of the club sat Noah. He was fucked up. He and one of his homeys smoked a blunt as they watched all the girls slowly wind and gyrate all over the place. Noah's eyes were half closed. Wafting smoke from the blunt formed a cloud above the table. Noah sang along to the song, loud as usual. He opened his eyes and damn near choked off the thick smoke. There she stood: chocolate, thick and beautiful. Her long, jet-black hair flowed down her back and she stared directly at him. Noah looked closer and realized that she was gesturing for him to come dance with her. He looked at his friend and said, "Damn flawless."

Noah could not turn this once in a lifetime opportunity down. The bitch was BAD!

Just as he started dancing with her, he noticed two drunken-ass niggas in the center of the club arguing. He tried to react but the haze had him on tilt. A 9mm nickel-plated gun rose above the crowd. Shots were fired and everyone started running and yelling. Noah held on to his newfound friend and headed for the exit.

Chapter 7

The Bitch is BACK

Ring, Ring, Ring.

Evea rolled over and looked at the clock with half-opened eyes. "Damn, who the hell calls someone on their first day back from vacation?" The time read 10:45 am. Evea had been asleep for a couple of hours longer than she planned. The phone continued ring. "Damn, where is TE`?"

"Hello?" Evea said in a stern whisper.

"Welcome back Bitch! Get your sleeping ass up! It's time to go out on the town! I am not about to waste my Saturday night because your tired ass want some rest. Shit, you rested enough for two weeks!"

Evea could not get a word in edgewise, "Tiff, slow the hell down!"

"The only thing I do slow is swallow a dick up. Come on with that slow shit. Get your ass up. I will be there to get you in thirty minutes! Bye!"

Evea tried to talk, "But Tiff…" The phone went dead.

Evea got out of the bed and began to get ready for her and Tiff's night out. She knew this would be a long night. Tiff had two weeks of gossip all saved up for Evea. Evea walked slowly into her large wall closet and sat on the chaise in the center of closet.

"What the hell am I going to wear tonight?" Evea spoke out loud to herself.

"Wear for what?" A voice shouted from the bathroom adjacent to the walk-in closet.

"There you are TE`! You scared me!" Evea said as she walked to the bathroom door. TE' was just closing the shower door. "Where are you going, mister?"

"Don't try that shit, Evea. I asked you that, remember?"

"Oh yeah, Tiff and I are going to some club."

"Now what about you?"

"I'm hooking up wit my niggas," he shouted above the steam and noise.

"Hurry up out of the shower. Tiff will be here any minute."

TE` licked his lips and responded, "Stop fronting and get in here with me. Let me get you right before you go out."

Evea's pussy was dripping pure sweet secretions of desire at the thought of TE`s hard dick with warm water running over it. She unsnapped her bra and pulled down her panties.

"Shit you don't have to tell me twice!" Evea got in the shower and TE` wasted no time reclining back. He kneeled down and let Evea sit on his face. Evea slid up and down real slow across TE`s stiff tongue. She held on to the shower door for support; her moans and screams of pure joy bounced off of the bathroom walls. Her cum, mixed with hot steaming water, ran down TE`s chin as he held her even closer to make sure she reached her highest peak. Evea turned around and touched the floor of the shower. TE` lifted her legs up backwards as she rested on her hands. He plunged so deep with the first stroke that he felt her pelvis bone. "Mmmm, man, you know I like it deep," Evea moaned louder.

TE` continued to pound that ass for thirty more minutes as they both got closer to climax. Evea's walls seemed to be pulling his dick in deeper and deeper with hard contractions. TE` knew when she was almost there. He sucked his index finger and stuck it straight up Evea's ass.

"OHHHHHHH SHIT!" she proclaimed, her body gyrating for at least five more minutes. They both sank down to the shower floor. Through all of their relationship problems their raw physical desire for each other remained unshaken.

Buzz, Buzz.

The doorbell rang. Evea ran around and tried to finish getting dressed. She ran and opened the door for Tiff. Tiff entered the house.

"Damn bitch, you ain't ready yet?"

TE` ran by Tiff and said, "What's up Tiff?"

"That's why your freaky ass ain't ready yet."

Evea smiled as she ran up the stairs to complete her primping and preening. A few minutes went by and Evea re-appeared, looking stunning.

"Oh shit, bitch, you glowing like the sun."

Evea wore a micro mini skirt showing off her long, pretty legs and an off-the-shoulder sweater and matching Sam and Libby knee boots. They were out for a night on the town.

"E, where did you cop that outfit? That shit is on fire!" Tiff said.

Evea stared into space. "I got this from a little strip in New York."

"What the fuck you looking so crazy for?" Tiff asked.

"I bought this to go to a concert with Adam."

Tiff looked at Evea with her hand on her hip. "Not tonight bitch, not tonight." They started laughing.

Tiff and Evea went to Club Sheik, one of their favorite spots to let loose. Nothing but ballers and bitches qualified to get ballers hung at Club Sheik. Evea and Tiff entered the club. Lights were flashing and niggas were definitely paying their way. They posted at the bar and the drinks were flowing like a roaring waterfall.

"Ahhhh shit, that's my shit," Evea said as she sang along with Kelis, ♫" I'M BOSSY I'M THE BITCH YAWL LOVE TO HATE, I'M THE BITCH WITH THE 808, CAUSE I'M BOSSY! I BROUGHT ALL THE BOYS TO THE YARD…." Evea got up and began to pop her ass and bounce all around; she was on the dance floor for four more songs. Tiff sat at the bar being cool like she normally did. She enjoyed seeing her friend have fun again.

The song played loudly, ♫ "Meet me in mall it's going down anywhere you meet me guaranteed to go down!"

TE` yelled, trying to hear over the loud bass line, "Hello!"

"What's up nigga?"

"Who this?"

"It's Noah nigga!"

TE' had to yell so loud, he was almost screaming. "Noah where you at? Why is the music so loud?"

"I'm in this club on South Street, Club Sheik! Guess who I just saw on the dance floor shaking her ass?"

"Who?"

"Evea, that's who."

"Yo, what the fucks are you doing in a damn club name Sheik? Why are not here at the Pussy Cat?"

"I'm wit my girl," Noah replied, sounding like a high-rollin' Vegas baller.

TE` raised his eyebrows and said in a high pitched voice, "Girl? Just one? You are missing all this good ass!" TE` continued, "Yo, good looking out on the phone call, but Evea is a grown-ass women, and we don't get down like that. Get your ass over here after you drop off that baggage. ONE."

TE` returned to his party with the fellas. He had one thing on his mind or one person, Butta. He thought about her for weeks since they last met. TE` was feeling good again. He and Evea had made a new connection on their vacation. Corn had taken care of his pick up while he was gone and the block was producing like hen houses again. He had enough work to keep the block thumping for a while. TE` was back in business!

"TE` who were you just tripping off on the phone?" Corn asked.

"Noah nut ass," TE' said. "He told me he was wit his girl. Who is this girl he's chillin' with now?"

"Damn, this bitch is bad. She's a chocolate sexy ass… He met her on New Year's at Club Abode. This nigga claims she was checking for him! He woke up the next morning in a hotel room SPRUNG! He has not let her out of his sight since then."

TE` sat there listening to every word, then broke his silence, "Where is she from?"

"I have never seen her around the hood," Corn replied. "I don't know, but I do know this Bitch is top grade "A" sirloin! She wouldn't even have to fuck me back. That bitch could just lay there and stare into space!"

TE` yelled out, "Ain't no bitch that bad!"

Evea stumbled back to the bar where Tiff was sitting and talking to two girls. Evea knew where that shit was headed. Tiff was a certified freak and did not hide it. She loved her toys- whether girls or boys.

"Tiff, guess who I saw over there in the corner? Noah and some girl."

"How did she look? Was she really dark?"

"Yeah, she's a pretty girl," Evea replied.

"I wouldn't mind tasting that shit myself."

"Tiff you crazy."

"No, I keeps it real 'Hood! He met her at the Club Abode a couple of weeks ago; yeah the club I almost got mirked at! I'm still mad about my fucking heel breaking on my four hundred dollar shoes!"

Evea laughed as she waved at Noah. He stood up and attempted to take Naih over to the bar to meet the girls. She stood up and said,

"Baby, I got to go to the little girl's room. I will find you when I come out."

Naih's phone rang as she entered the bathroom. "Yo, Ziggy!"

"Stop playing, Naih," Zayne yelled from the other end of her phone. "Where are you, sexy?"

"I'm out with Noah. Why are you calling me now?"

"My bad, sexy, hit me back when you get off work!" Zayne's quick tongue replied.

"Zig…" The phone went dead. Naih said to herself, "No this nigga did not bang on me!"

Chapter 8

Dangerous Curves

The day was cold and blustery. Adam stepped out of his condo and he was chilled to the bone. He could see his breath escaping from his lungs. He looked down at his watch impatiently awaiting his car to be pulled up. The valet pulled the car around and he hurried up to the driver's door.

He slipped the valet a twenty and said, "Good looking out" as he drove off. Adam was on the hunt;

he was still checking out the nigga's profiles that Zayne gave him. He was not having much luck. He was also trying to find out who was checking for him. He still had no clue as to who wanted him dead. This shit had him fucked up. Adam flipped his cell phone open and began to dial Evea's number. He hoped this time she would talk to him. Her answering machine came on. "Shit!" he said out loud.

He hung up and called Butta. "Yo, what's up little sis?"

"Nothing, what's up with you?"

"Shit. I wanted to hook up for lunch at the spot," Adam said.

"All right, ONE," Butta replied.

Adam proceeded to head to the restaurant. As he went through a red light, his chirp sounded.

"What's up nigga? You solo?"

Adam knew that could only be one person, Zayne. "Yeah what's up?"

"How are you coming along with that project?"

"I'm still working on it," Adam replied.

"Right, Right. I got an inside man on it; or should I say woman. We should know something soon."

Adam was not in favor of trusting Zayne's inside connect, which was indicated by his lack of response.

"I know you don't trust no bitch!" Zayne hollered, then toning his voice down to speak his truth. "Nigga, I got this: Naih is the best that ever did it, you just keep your ear to the street. I'll handle this shit." Before Adam could respond, Zayne gave him his exit. "ONE."

Rizz and Sin rode down 21st Street. They got caught at the light. Sin yelled, "Damn! Where the fuck did that car come from?" A sleek and shiny Jaguar sped pass them and made the light. They drove a few more blocks up and noticed the Jag had parked in front of Bon Apetite restaurant.

Rizz, who was always ready and willing to get caught up with a new bitch said, "That probably was a fine-ass female in that car. You know bitches can't drive." As soon as he said it, a pretty, golden-yellow female emerged from the restaurant and went to get something from that car. "Damn she's bad. Yo Sin, we have to ride back through after we handle this business."

"Nigga you pressed," Sinsere said. "That bitch could be with somebody- you not thinking straight."

Rizz gave him a sideways look and said with an attitude, "That nigga ain't my people. I don't give a fuck, just spin back through and watch me do what I do!"

Sinsere laughed at his bravado and said sarcastically, "What do you do?"

The light changed and they drove off.

Sinsere pulled up and parked in front of a fire hydrant. That was just like him- impatient and too lazy to find a real parking spot for fear of having to walk too far. That explained his husky build. Sinsere was brown skinned and a little on the chunky side. That did not stop his flow with the ladies. They often referred to him as "Big Sexy." He always was dressed to impress seven days a week and smelt good enough to eat. Sinsere stepped out of the car and brushed off his fresh lay. Rizz was often annoyed by his brother's GQ attitude. He yelled out, "Nigga just come on, we going to meet Lex, not a truck load of bitches!"

They approached the Irish Pub and still did not see any signs of Lex. The temperature, accompanied by their appetites, forced them inside of O'Hymen's Pub, located deep in South Philly where most of the Irish and Italians in the city lived.

A petite redhead greeted them. "May I help you? How many in your party?"

"Three," Rizz responded, never looking in her face because he was too occupied with the size of her breasts.

"Damn, she got some big twins to be her size!" Sinsere laughed at his brother's loud, rude nature. Lex arrived fifteen minutes after they were seated.

"What up my niggas? Y'all couldn't wait a couple more minutes?" Lex called out as he took a seat.

Rizz laughed and said, "You know this fat mutherfucker was hungry."

Adam and Butta sat and talked about old times. They laughed about how they were raised and joked about the time when they both faked the Holy Ghost so they would be excused from prayer meeting. They both looked at each other and said, "Look what we're doing now!"

"So, you heard anything about Manny's murder yet?" Butta asked.

"No, but I still got my ear to the streets. The streets just the fuck ain't talking. But Lil' sis, I can't talk to you about the shit me and my squad is into. That shit is confidential."

Butta leaned back in her chair and tossed her long hair over her left shoulder. "Yeah whatever, stop acting like I don't live in these streets! I know how shit go."

Adam put his hands up in the air as if he was being stuck up, "Go ahead, you fake ass gangsta." They both cracked up laughing.

Lex called the meeting with his nephews to strategically plan how to flush Adam out of hiding. Rizz and Sinsere did not buy Lex's theory that Adam was still alive. They thought he was being paranoid. But Lex told them that it was too strange that there was no news report about anybody in a car being shot or killed, and that the car just disappeared.

They continued to talk about who Adam used to chill with and where he chilled. They were going to make some surprise visits to the spots. Lex explained that he would be back in Philly on business in a few more days and would meet up with them then.

Butta and Adam were done lunch and headed to the front of the restaurant. Butta forgot her cell phone and had to go back to the table. One of her female friends was blowing her phone up. Adam sat at the front of the restaurant in a chestnut brown wooden chair. He thought to himself how much fun he had with Butta, just like old times. Butta appeared at the front door and Adam stood up to exit the building. Butta walked ahead of Adam making fun of his walk. Rizz and Sinsere drove by and saw Butta. Rizz was pointing to the golden beauty and asking Sin to stop the car. Rizz leaned out of the window and whistled at Butta. Adam had dropped his keys and was bending over to pick them up. Butta turned around to see her caller. They met eyes and she flashed her smile at him. At this point Adam stood up and Sinsere, Rizz and Adam caught eyes simultaneously.

Rizz yelled, "OHHH SHIT! There that nigga go, slow down."

Adam dove for the car door as shots rained down over he and Butta's head. Adam was concerned about his little sis. He was trying to make it back to his back seat where his stash of weapons was. Adam didn't know little sis *was really* a rider!

"Stay the fuck on the ground," Butta yelled.

She spun around and lifted up her tea -length suede skirt and pulled a Lady Wesson 9mm out of a thigh holster and came up dumping back. Adam's eyes were full of pure shock.

"What the fuck?" he said under his breath.

Butta hit Rizz in the upper torso. Adam made it to the car and came out blazing a chrome-plated Desert Eagle. Sinsere pulled off fast when he noticed that Butta had hit his brother.

Butta and Adam drove off as news vans were pulling up in front of Bon Appetite.

"What the fuck was that about!" Butta questioned Adam.

Adam looked at Butta for a moment, then asked, "Where the fuck did you learn that Rambo shit?"

Butta looked back at him, eyes open wide as she dusted off her skirt and licked her finger to clean off a spot of dirt on her shirt. "I told you I was street. One of my many thug men taught me how to shoot and shit."

"Remind me to thank that nigga," Adam said as he tucked his Armani into his Calvin Klein's.

Adam now knew exactly who was after him and he figured out that they were the ones who shot Evea or had something to do with the shooting. Adam could not get the surprised look on Sinsere and Rizz's faces out of his mind. He went over and over in his head and thought, "Those niggas was not following me; they thought I was dead." Adam knew that this old feud had to come to an end and *he* had to be the one to end it. He vowed to himself that this time he wouldn't do any more half-assed jobs. Sin and Rizz hurt a woman he adored for the last time. This time the revenge would be double sweet: for Evea and his mother.

Chapter 9

Reunited

Evea returned to work on Monday well rested and ready for a new chapter in her life. She was finally feeling like herself again and was healing mentally as well as physically. Evea sat at her desk and checked her messages. She had several hang up messages left on her voice mail. She didn't think anything of it at the time.

Evea saw several clients and was very busy. She took a break for a moment and decided to go to the bathroom to regroup. As she turned the corner, she could see the brick-red steel doors with white numbers on them. She passed a well lit office encased in a wall of glass. A new face occupied the Lieutenant's office. She wondered where Lieutenant Bricks was. He never took many days off, and he definitely did not like anyone else in his office.

Evea entered her office frantically as the phone rang, "Hello, Mrs. Jordan speaking."

"What's up girl!" a voice shouted on the phone.

"Tiff? Oh my goodness, I'm not dealing with no bitch today?"

"Look bitch, nobody can't be nice to you. What are you doing?"

"I'm still high from that good time we had at the club the other night! I'm feeling all new and shit!" Evea explained.

"Yo, Tiff what happened to your jump off?"

"Who? Rubby?"

"Yeah, you know who I'm talking about."

"Oh, you didn't hear about that shit," Tiff responded in a nonchalant manner.

"Tiff what did you do?"

"Why I had to be involved with that shit?" Tiff said with a giggle. "Anyway, he was caught on camera with one of the gay inmates with his head in his crotch or at least that is how it looked to the warden. He won't be returning to work or to his house!"

"Oh shit, are you serious?" Evea said.

"Let's see him talk about that sexy young thing he's fucking now!"

"Tiff, you are a spawn of the devil!"

"No, I'm not. I'm just nobody to fuck with!"

Evea packed up her things and prepared to go home. She placed all of the reports that she needed to complete in the proper bin. She turned the lights out in her office and thanked God for letting her make it through another day at the prison unharmed. She walked through all of the checkpoints and finally made it to the front parking lot. Evea was dressed warm to fight the chill in the air. It had turned colder and colder as the winter season moved along. She wore a black pair of corduroy jeans and a cream color cashmere sweater. Her hair was in a bun and she modeled a matching heather gray pea coat and boots. As she approached her jeep she fumbled with her keys to unlock the door and start the car. She reached the driver's side door and a man with a black skully and a heavy luxurious winter coat stepped from behind her car. She was startled. Evea dropped all of her papers and purse onto the ground. All she could do was stand there as tears flowed down her face. There Adam stood, looking as sexy as she could remember. This was the first time they had seen each other since the shooting and the loss of their child. The long time they'd been apart melted away to mere moments.

"Sunshine, it's really you?" Adam said as he reached out to touch her cheek to wipe her tears.

"I missed you so much! I know I shouldn't have come here, but I couldn't bear being away from you another day. Look, shit has gotten real, and I don't know how much longer I have on this earth. I just know I could not leave this world with out giving you your props. Evea, I LOVE YOU, like I have never loved anyone in this world. I know us together is wrong because you are already spoken for, but that does not erase the real shit we share between us."

Tears flowed out of Evea's eyes like a broken faucet. Every emotion she had ever felt for Adam was present at that exact moment. She interrupted his speech and said: "Adam, I LOVE YOU more than I can express in words; but I also LOVE my husband whom I am devoted to. I won't leave him, I can't…" Evea believed what she was saying, but whether she felt it in her heart was another question.

Adam stopped her. The words he never wanted to hear had just stabbed his eardrums, making them bleed red rivers of sorrow. "Sunshine, I understand- but that does not change what we have. Can you take a ride with me for old time sake? I need to show you something and have a chance to speak from my heart."

Evea stood there; she knew the right thing but she couldn't betray her heart. She cut her jeep off and climbed in the passenger side of Adam's plush Jaguar. Adam's system quaked classic 2Pac all the way up the highway as he sang along,

♫ ALL I NEED IN THIS WORLD TODAY IS ME AND MY GIRLFRIEND!..."

The air seemed to get colder the further they got up state PA. Evea looked out the window, reminiscing about the last time they were at the spot. Adam drove up to a huge house that was up the road from the place he had shown Evea months ago.

"Adam, what are we doing here?"

He didn't answer. He just stopped the car and got out to open her door and escorted Evea up to the house. The house was stunning, there were at least twelve bedrooms and acres of land with livestock. Two pure white horses were grazing at the front of the gate. The front entrance had double cherry wood hand carved doors. When Adam opened the door with a key, Evea's breathing became uneven.

The house was fully furnished and was a dream come true. Evea was overcome with emotion. Adam looked at her and began to stroke her hair, then he kissed her neck, slowly and softly, blowing on her skin ever so slightly before his lips touched her skin. Evea was feeling so good, higher than any drug could take her. They were back at it again. They grabbed each other, kissed and sucked. Evea climaxed five times and Adam's was still rock hard. She mounted him and took all of him in slowly. After they were exhausted and all but out of liquid, they lay there looking at the shimmering evening sky through the skylight.

Adam explained to Evea that he knew why she was shot and who did it. He also explained that he was about to go to war with the niggas and he might not make it out alive. Evea was not prepared to really live in this world without Adam. Adam let her know that the house was in her name for her to do whatever she wanted to do with it. It was his hopes- his dying wish-that she used the house for a getaway when she needed to be close to him- in the event he was not victorious in the war.

Chapter 10

Hide and Seek

`Lex's phone vibrated, "What up Son?"

"Yo Lex, you were right that nigga is still alive. We were just in a shootout with him and some bitch. Rizz was hit pretty bad. I had to take him to the hospital."

"Yo son, do what you have to do then call and let me know what's what."

"What that nigga driving?" Lex questioned Sin.

"A silver Jag," Sin replied.

"I got you, ONE."

Lex planned to handle him right this time. He could not understand how the mutherfucka was still walking around after all of the shots up close. He began to believe that he hit the wrong car or the wrong person! This time he was not going to miss.

Lex was on the highway by now, but he had not gotten far. Lex hit the next exit and proceeded to the nearest rest stop to make some calls. He sat there in the car- mad at himself for slipping. He did not do his homework right. Among his many calls to rearrange some business, he called Tiff. He needed some stress relief badly and knew that Tiff was just the one to give it to him.

Rizz arrived at the hospital and was rushed into surgery. He had lost a lot of blood and his right shoulder had a hole in it the size of a quarter. The doctors worked feverishly on his wounds. The sterile operating room was full of qualified surgeons who were used to seeing young men come in the hospital all broken up and shot to pieces from street violence. Most of the doctors were from upper class suburban areas and worked in the inner-city ER a couple times a week, just to feel like they "gave back".

There was a loud beeping sound coming from one of the machines. Rizz flat-lined twice. The doctors were about to give up. But one of the head operating room nurses gave a brief and powerful speech. She reminded them all that Rizz was very special to some people, and no matter how he sustained his injuries he deserved the same treatment as any other patient. Before the nurse finished speaking her mind, one of the doctors began CPR while the crash cart was being prepared. The nurse yelled, "CLEAR!" and everybody stepped away from the table. Rizz's body convulsed.

"We have a pulse!" another doctor said enthusiastically. The concerned nurse stood there and observed the situation, thanking God for the people that had helped her daughter survive a similar situation not long ago.

Rizz was out of the operating room and in recovery when the doctor approached Sinsere, who stood there in disbelief as the doctor explained the extent of Rizz's injuries. He had no idea that his brother was so close to death.

Lex had just come from a much-needed 'meeting' with Tiff. He was relaxed and refreshed. Tiff gave him one of her fuck-the-stress-away specials. Lex was in the streets and searching for the silver Jag. He was ready to open fire on the nigga as soon as he saw him. Sinsere had called him and let him know that Rizz almost lost his arm and his life and this did nothing but infuriate him. He went down to "The Point," a hip strip in Philly where everybody hung out, even during the winter months. He canvassed the place for a silver Jag and came up with nothing. Lex had gotten so desperate that he was even willing to look for the bitch that was with Adam to fish him out. He walked by gangs of people standing around watching the daring souls do tricks on their 4x4. Bitches stood around cheering and dick riding, hoping to get sported by one of the riders. Restless and full of frustration, Lex ended up at a nearby bar drinking shots of Hennessey. His mind wandered off to the thought of his nephew dying and his sister snapping! He thought to himself, "This shit has to be done. It's more than personal now." As Lex sat at the bar drowning in cognac he noticed a stunning creature enter the bar. "Damn!" he said aloud without noticing the nigga she had on her arm. He looked closer to the guy that was in tow. It was Noah, TE`s cousin.

Lex approached him and gave him some dap. "What up Son?"

"Yo, what the fuck you doing in here?" Noah replied.

"I'm in here on some chill shit and possibly some business," Lex said.

Noah sat down at the bar and gestured for Naihira to go sit at a booth while he talked to Lex. Noah was not feeling the fact that Lex was scoping her; he did not mix business with pleasure. Naihira told Noah that she was going to the restroom.

Noah continued to discuss business with Lex. Noah let him know that his product was doing the damn thing down the end and that TE` would be in contact with him soon. Noah and Lex did not know each other and they quickly ran out of conversation. Soon Noah became worried and told Lex that he would get at him later, he was going to check on Naih and make sure she was cool.

Noah made his way through the crowded and dimly lit bar. He finally reached the back of the bar and in the left hand corner was a small brown door with a man and woman sign hung on it. He saw no sign of Naih, but the restroom door was closed. Noah sat in a dark corner at an empty table, hoping to catch Naih as she came out of the restroom so they could get a drink and leave. The place was too packed to enjoy the atmosphere. Noah, thought to himself, "I can't even let off shots if I have to- there's too many niggas in this place."

A couple of shots of Patrone and ten minutes later, Naih appeared in the restroom door and stepped to the right of the room with her cell phone still in her hand. She was less than ten feet from Noah, but she couldn't see him in the shadow. He was about to reach out and touch her when he heard her whispering.

"Look nigga, this shit ain't cool. Stop calling me while I am working.... what! I got that nigga under control and I will have your information soon. What about Adam?"

Noah just sat there watching the gorgeous creature say ugly things into her cell. Noah had heard enough. His first instinct was to blast the bitch were she stood. Noah could not take another syllable of Naih's deceitful plan, so he slid out of the shadow and said in a your-my-baby voice, "Hey sweetie, who you talking too?"

Naih stood there stunned, wondering where he came from. She acted as if she did not here him and spoke into the phone; "All right Mom, I have to go."

"Talkin' to your Mother so late? What a good little girl."

Noah had heard enough to seal her fate, but she was too hot to let go that easy. He kissed her on the neck and said, "Sexy, let's get out of here. I got something for you." Noah, being the dog he was, had to taste that juicy ass one more time.

Noah and Naihira left the club and headed for one of the more hood-like motels. Noah's excuse was that he left his stacks in the house by mistake. He hated slimy niggas or bitches and he could not bring himself to spend any more money on Naih after what he had just heard. They arrived at the motel and Noah was cocked and ready to go. He could not wait to give Naih what she needed- not the love she expected.

They entered the room and Noah started by undressing her. Once she was naked he proceeded to grab her aggressively and bite on her neck and back. Noah slid her head down to his crotch and when he could feel her breath on the tip of his dick he slammed her face down on it. He pounded her face like a newly released convict getting his first piece of ass on the street. Naih tried to gasp for air but Noah's hard gun kept blazing. He finally let Naih up for air and she said, "Nigga you ready for me tonight, huh?"

In mid sentence he grabbed her and bent her over facing the raggedy headboard. Noah rammed his dick so far up inside of her that she let out a loud roar. He pounded her from the back as he pulled her hair and spanked her ass. Naih was enjoying herself until he pulled out and shoved his brick hard manhood in her ass. Tears flowed down her face as she took one for her team. Noah realized that his anger was reaching the point of no return and he pulled out. Naih lay there with a bleeding ass wondering where did that beast come from. Noah would never be gentle with her again. He made his mind up to fuck her thug-style from that day forth.

Chapter 11

Unspoken desires

Ring ,Ring, Ring.

TE` hurried to the other side of the family room to quickly find the house phone. "Where the hell is this phone?" He finally found the cordless phone and dove to the floor to catch it before the person on the other end hung up.

"Hello," TE` said.

A voice on the other end greeted him with a string of questions, "What's up cousin? Why are you still in the house? We need to handle some business. I found out some shit that you need to hear and that I need some direction on." Noah wasn't in the mood for small talk.

"Look dog, I hear all that, but if it is not an emergency- I am in for the day. I got in this morning from hanging out."

"Nigga this is an emergency. It is about that nut-ass nigga Adam and company!"

"All right, I got you, I will be there," TE' replied, sensing the situation needed handling.

"Be where nigga?"

"Meet me at Lucky Sal's on 10th and South."

"All right, ONE!"

TE` threw Evea a bullshit excuse why he had to leave the house. Kayla was slowly moving back in with them after the shooting and they were going to have a lazy day. They both had agreed to do the family thing and stay in. TE` quickly got ready. He was dressed in all black denim accompanied by black three quarter length Timberlands and a leather jacket so soft, when touched, it left fingerprints on it. His mind raced and his adrenaline pumped. He kissed Evea and Kayla goodbye and grabbed his keys to his black 2006 Magnum, equipped with chrome "spinnas" and chrome hardware.

Lucky Sal's was packed. When TE` drove up and there were no parking spaces left in self-parking, TE` got out of the car and tossed the keys to the valet. His car was one of many waiting to be parked. It was a mid March night and cold enough to see your breath; but the hope of spring coming was right around the corner. South Street was lively and everywhere the eye could see was littered with people trying to get in the latest club or lounge. Sal's was different. You had to possess a platinum key that was scanned at the front door for authenticity. Sal's was owned by one of the few real blood Italian mafia. Sal's was definitely an exclusive club. TE` had done some construction work for big Sal and he liked it so much that he gave TE` and his crew unlimited use of the private club.

TE` entered Sal's and looked around for Noah. He saw many people sitting around admiring the featured act. She was a half black and half Cambodian beauty. She was fully exposed as she did tricks on the straight chrome pole. TE` made his way to the back of the bar and still saw no sign of Noah. It was not like Noah to be late, so TE` began to think harder. It dawned on him where Noah was. TE` got out of his plush velvet seat and walked toward the side of the bar. As he approached the heavy, gigantic doors, a huge bald-headed guy interrupted his stride. TE` reached in his wallet and pulled out his player's card. The bald, husky man scanned it and stepped aside as the doors opened.

TE` spotted Noah at the first table. Lights were flashing and beautiful girls were plentiful. Loud voices filled the air and bounced off the thirty-foot high hand carved ceiling. There Noah sat with a model-looking girl on his lap. He had several multi-color gambling chips in front of him adding up to $100,000. TE` walked up to him and tapped him on the shoulder. Noah slid his 45 out of the holster and turned around all in one motion.

TE` looked at him, smiled and said, "That's my nigga!"

Noah laughed and said, "You was almost the nigga; the nigga that got shot!"

They gave each other a pound and began to talk business.

Noah told TE` about what he had overheard Naihira saying on the phone. Noah explained that he heard her say Adam's name and some other nigga's name that began with a Z. TE` sat there taking in all of the information. He questioned Noah: "Where do you think she knows Adam from? Do you think she is spying on us for him? And if so, why?"

Noah answered yes to all of TE`'s questions. One thing Noah did not know was why Naihira was on him; but what he did know was she would be sorry for it. TE` told Noah to plant false info and see where it led them. TE` knew that Manny's right-hand man's name was Zayne, and that was too coincidental that the nigga's name that Noah could not hear correctly began with a Z. TE` had a feeling that somehow Manny and his crew and Adam was connected. This seemed far-fetched. But nothing in the hood was impossible!

The night was winding down. TE` and Noah had won thousands of dollars and put thousands back on the table. Noah won back $75,000; he was definitely up. TE` won $10,000 and lost $3,000. TE` tried to convince Noah it was time to go. After Noah finished his Cuban cigar they both went their separate ways. Noah knew his task and he had just the right bait in mind. He knew since fucking him was a job for Naih she would be on call whenever he needed her.

TE` got in his Magnum and headed toward home. He passed by several clubs and the let-outs were crazy. He saw bitches from everywhere; all in different flavors and shades like a Tastycake factory. He drove up on the corner of 8th and South and noticed that Butta was walking to her car alone. He rode up on her in a sly manner. He just sat there staring as her ass jiggled with each step. He said jokingly, "Going my way?"

Butta turned around and saw who was flirting with her and the glow of her smile competed with the moonlight. "That depends. Are you stalking me?" she replied.

"No, I'm admiring you!"

Butta looked at him and wanted him even more.

"In that case, follow me mystery man!"

Butta entered her car as TE` had thoughts about entering Butta.

TE` and Butta arrived at her downtown apartment. They could feel the heat rising between them like steam from a subway vent.

TE watched Butta's ass sway from left to right as she lead him to the private entrance of her love den. His mouth began to water as it did at the smell of his mother's fried chicken. They reached the top of the stairs and did not waist any time. Butta's apartment was exactly how TE` imagined it. Her bedroom was a scene out of a love story. The silk flowing curtains swayed to the vibration of the blowing heat. He grabbed her by the top of her denim skirt and pulled her close enough to feel her soft body against his. Butta did not expect to get things poppin' so fast; but she did not resist. TE` undressed her like a scene going in slow motion. He could not wait to consume her like his last meal. He slid her skirt off gently and stood there admiring her perfectly put together frame. Off went her blouse and bra, exposing her pretty, perky breasts with nipples the color of honey. As he sucked each nipple slow and hard he watched her legs tremble with excitement. Butta wanted some more interaction. She arched her body up toward TE`, begging to be completely taken. TE` felt this energy and plugged into her unspoken request. He spread her legs apart and while sucking on both nipples he gently rubbed the tip of her clit making her jerk with anticipation. Butta was unfamiliar to TE` but that did not stop him from diving in head first and sucking Butta's snatch until it squirted creamy clouds of joy. TE` set up for the home run: his big hands palmed her ass as he prepared for his first stroke when … Ring, Chirp, Ring.

Butta's phone rang with a signal for an urgent call and she had to answer it. "Hello?" She said, still trying to catch her breath.

"What you doing Sis?" he said in a slurred speech pattern.

"Damie this shit better be important," she whispered in a stern voice. TE` looked as if that name was familiar. He couldn't believe he just heard that name uttered with the woman who was about to ride him to heaven. It had to be a coincidence? He wondered until he saw her hard nipples protruding from her stout breasts.

Butta saw TE`s face and felt his distraction. She apologized for the call and excused herself and went in the bathroom. TE' looked at her naked ass shake all the way to the light of the bathroom.

It was Adam calling to get some comfort after being out on a drinking binge. Butta set him straight and quickly returned to bed. She brought him to full mast again and they set sail on the rocking ocean.

Chapter 12

Bloody WAR

Bang, Bang, Bang. The door swung open and an odd-looking, short dark skinned guy came to the door. As he cracked the door just enough to see out he was met with an AK -47.

"GIVE THAT SHIT UP PUSSY!" Adam yelled. The guy seemed to be stunned and tried to run away from the door. Adam rushed into the half-lit row house and ready for whatever. This was a known spot that Rizz and Sinsere had their hands in, and he wanted them to know he meant business. This was definitely war; and in any war, there had to be a winner and a loser. The wars that go on in the street were just like the wars going on overseas. Some might say the street wars were worse. To lose the street war meant nothing but death. There was no negotiating in street wars. There would be death in both crews and there wasn't a damn thing anybody could do to stop it. No politics could prevent the bloodshed that lay ahead. Rizz and Sinsere had started the war years prior and they were going to be in it until no one was left standing!

Adam pointed the gun in the man's face and demanded that he give up all the cash and drugs. The guy tried to reason with him and tell him he had nothing else to give. Adam did not go for that shit so he placed the gun in the guy's mouth and said, "Nigga, you gone die about this money and this work?"

A $100,000 dollars in cash sat on the table with half bagged up coke on another table in the kitchen. Three guys sat in brown recliners in the far left corner of the living room.

"Get the fuck up and let me see all y'all hands, niggas!"

They all stood up, and one would be hero attempted to reach for the sawed-off shotie under the coffee table. It was a fact that the men outnumbered Adam by three, or so they thought!

As the tall, high-yellow pretty boy reached, a loud sound rang out…Boooooomb! The basement door swung open and out ran Zayne blazing first and questioning later. He lit each one of the three guys up! The pretty boy fell, bloody, humped over the brown chair with the gun still in his hand. The short guy that Adam had corned began pleading for his life! Zayne said, almost with a touch of sympathy for the poor fool: "Look nigga, I saw the safe in the basement. Either you get down and give up the combo or nigga you gone lay down and I'll figure the combo out with my gun."

He folded under pressure; that nigga sung like a new member on the church choir. Zayne and Adam gathered all the stash and left a blood bath behind. The block was on volcano mode.

It was a cold and windy evening in March. Sinsere struggled to push pass the wind as he walked up the poorly lit, small city street. He was on his way to pick up his weekly cut from one of he and his brother's many drug houses. With his brother recovering, he was left to do a lot of pick-ups alone. Lex was not going to assist him because he was the ghost of the crew. He kept it that way to allow himself access anywhere. As he got closer to the house his phone rang. Sinsere stopped in front of the house to answer his phone. It was one of his many hoes.

"Look sweetheart, I'm gone hit you after I take care of this business."

Sinsere walked up the steps laughing at the girl's comments. As he approached the door he saw no signs of any movement. He knocked on the front door hard. No one answered; he reached in the small of his back and gathered his 18-karat white gold-plated 9mm.

Sin eased the door open and saw bodies everywhere. "OH Shit!" he yelled.

The house was completely cleaned out and all of his soldiers were gone. The only thing that remained was a black leather purse sitting on the table in the dining area. Sinsere picked it up and knew instantly what that symbolized. "ADAM!" He said loudly. Adam had left the purse to let them know who was there. The purse was a slap in the face and a little something to remind them of that cold fall day years ago when he and his brother robbed Adam's mom. Sinsere stood there fucked up over all the bloodshed and confirmed that Adam had to go.

Zayne and Adam pulled off in different cars and agreed to meet up at their spot to count the money and work up. Zayne arrived first and sat there waiting for Adam. He wondered why he was just involved in that shit. He never even asked Adam how he heard about them niggas having money and work like that. He started to think there was more to the story than Adam was telling him!

Adam called Zayne and told him he ran into a little trouble and would catch him later. Zayne really was suspicious now. He thought, "I hope I don't have to rock this nigga before it's all over."

As Zayne sat there counting his stash his phone rang. "What up?" he answered.

A sexy voice on the other end replied, "You… in a little while."

"For real."

"Sexy, I got some news that I think you should know. You got time later on?"

"Naih, I got time now, come over so I can feel your naked body on all this cash!"

"Say no more," she replied in a sultry whisper.

Naih came out of the bathroom and had to make up an excuse to leave Noah. Noah had not even got in the drawls yet and she was planning on leaving. She was still getting over their last encounter.

Noah was getting off the phone when Naih emerged from the shower. He asked her what took her so long in the shower. She made up an excuse that she was not feeling so well and needed to leave. Naih liked dick as much as the next bitch; but she loved Zayne's dick. It was a difference with her. She did not want to fuck Noah and risk being too hurt to ride that big chocolate thunder that Zayne possessed. Just the thought of her being with him made her drip creamy pearls. Naih loved Zayne and would do anything for him for a price.

Noah sat there staring at Naih wanting to take her out right there. He could not stand sneaky bitches; because he needed her alive and not hurt infuriated him. He calmed himself down by sparking up an L.

"I got you after I finish this L. I'll drop you off at your car." Noah finished his L and did as he said he would, having to hold off the urge to bust a cap in her and dump her in the Delaware.

As soon as she got out of the car Noah called TE`. "Yo Cousin! She fell for the bait. Slimy ass bitch probably on her way to meet with them niggas right now!"

"That is what slimy bitches do," TE' replied.

"Yo, where you at? I called you and…"

TE` interrupted him: "I got to tell about that shit much later! ONE."

Chapter 13

Harsh Reality

Lex had been looking for Adam for weeks. He had the hunger of a brown grizzly coming out of hibernation. He was furious with Adam and his fucking BALLS to run up in his nephew's house and kill up all his crew like he did. Lex's hunt for Adam had him coming back to the city more often. That meant him seeing Tiff more often. He also was able to drop off some shit for TE`. This visit was no different. Tiff lay next to Lex, fast asleep.

The sun was breaking through the thick beautiful drapes that hung from the top of the 14-foot high ceiling. The bed consumed Tiff's small frame. She was sleeping off a night of Grade-A over the top fucking! Lex could not leave that pussy alone if he wanted to. Tiff was a sexual beast and did shit to Lex that no one else had ever done. She kept gadgets and new tricks working on a regular basis. Her latest trick damn near killed Lex. Tiff drank ice-cold water before she gave Lex head. She drank three glasses back to back until her throat was numb. She sat him in a straight back chair and tied his wrist to the chair and his ankles to the legs. Tiff slid down between his legs and slowly swallowed his dick like it was a prescription pill. Up and down she went on his hammer until her lips touched his pelvic bone. Lex stared at her in amazement as she kissed his pubic hair with each downward motion. Her tonsils tickled the tip of his dick and brought him closer to climax. Tiff felt the jerking and she knew what that meant. She stood up and placed the strap-on bullet on her Clit, set it to high, and mounted his big dick from the back. Lex screamed and shook as his dick disappeared in Tiff's ass. Tiff bounced up and down on his dick like he was in her frontal area. Lex was speechless. He began to shake and moan louder and louder. The chair sounded as if it was going to brake in half. She finally hit the right spot and they both came so hard that Lex ripped the arms off of the chair as Tiff's white creamy juices ran down his legs.

Tiff rolled over and noticed Lex staring at her. "Damn nigga, why you stalking a bitch while I'm asleep?"

Lex never replied, he just gave her his sexy grin and half laugh. Tiff got up and began to gather her belongings to take to the hotel bathroom.

"So, what's up for the day?" Tiff asked.

"Well, I got business to handle. You can take the car and the credit card and I will meet up wit ya later."

"You only have to tell me to take the card once!"

Lex smacked Tiff on the ass as she switched to the bathroom to shower.

While Tiff was in the shower Lex thought that he would try to handle some small shit over the phone. He heard Tiff trying to sing and figured she was all ready in the shower. He called Sinsere and Rizz. Rizz was almost fully recovered and he was rolling with his brother again.

"What up Son? Did you get that kid Adam yet?"

"Yo, I can't believe he is still walking the fuck around. I won't miss that pussy this time. I'll check the car this time," Sinsere said.

Tiff was on her way to get her shower cap and she overheard the conversation. Tiff 's entire body was numb. She was hoping that this was a coincidence. She was definitely ruthless and did not care about bloodshed when someone fucked with any of her people. Tiff decided to ease back in the bathroom and not mention what she overheard at least until she did some further investigation of her own.

Tiff went shopping and eased her mind with Gucci and Prada. She decided to call Evea and ask her to meet her at the mall. Evea agreed to come and keep her company. Tiff was determined to investigate without letting Evea know what was going on.

Ring, Ring, Ring.

"Yeah!" Evea answered.

"Dam bitch, what's up with you?"

"Nothing, what's up with you Tiff?"

"I was just calling to see how far you are…"

"I'm almost there- why you on my back, bitch?" Evea said.

"Oh, I guess you on a drought again… that's why you so cranky!"

"I told your ass to come to the sex show with me and get some act right! Because when a nigga won't, my bullet 2000 will!"

"Tiff, you are absolutely fucked up in the head!"

"NO! I'm constantly fucked any way I want to be fucked! Just hurry your nut-ass up before the stores close!"

"Ain't no damn stores closing this early," Evea said.

"Shit, if I'm in here any longer with this credit card they are going to have to close from empty shelves!" Tiff always wanted to get the last word in.

Tiff stood by the entrance near Gucci at King of Prussia mall. Evea walked in and took over the scene. She was draped in the finest Versace burnt orange silk dress with matching blazer. Her feet were covered with hand-embroidered brown Gucci boots and a yellow oversized Gucci bag. Evea stayed in all of the fashion magazines and made sure she was right for each season. With spring fast approaching she was right in line with the colors. The groundhog had predicted an early spring, so winter would only be lasting a couple of more weeks. Tiff walked up to her, dressed casual and comfortable for shopping. Tiff wore dark denim jeans and a matching jacket with 2in money green Prada boots. They hugged as they gave a mutual, "What's up?" Tiff could tell something was wrong with Evea and she figured she better get it out of the way before she started questioning her about the day of the shooting.

Evea broke the silence: "You know that nigga did not come home last night! He did not even call. He has been acting strange lately and I thought we were cool!"

"Niggas ain't never cool, especially when they know somebody else been poking around in their shit! They think they are the only ones that can be sexually free," Tiff said.

"You know how I feel: FUCK EM! As long as I have a pulse… I'm going to fuck who I want, when I want! Oh I forgot- and where I want!" They both fell out laughing.

They walked and talked about bullshit and practically bought out the mall. Evea told Tiff.

"Tiff you are not going to believe this shit. I saw Adam again," Evea said casually.

"WHAT!" Tiff screamed. Bitch, you beyond Fifty Cent, you a fucking mental client! You crazy. And you had me all upset about TE` staying out and you still fucking around with Rico Suave!"

"It kinda just happened as a farew…."

Tiff interrupted her and said, "I thought getting lit the fuck up in his car was farewell enough!" Tiff used the opportunity to question Evea about the shooting. "So E, did you get a look at the shooter or his car?"

"Yeah, of his car; but why you ask me that?"

"I was thinking about shit, that's all."

"Yeah his car was black with really dark tint. Looked something like a Lexus or Acura."

Tiff had her answer. She started going over the time frame of the shooting and the time that Lex was supposed to meet with her that day. She was falling hard for Lex and now she had an obligation to either tell TE` this info about the shooter or to handle this shit herself. She was definitely a boss and not scared of shit; but her emotions for him were a roadblock. She thought about letting TE` handle it, but she did not know if TE` would have the right connects because he was not on the streets any more- so she thought.

Chapter 14

Blooming Revenge

Spring was in the air and all was bright and cheery. The first day of spring topped out at a record 89 degrees. It seemed funny that it was so cold just two weeks prior to spring beginning. People hurried in the streets and dressed in bright spring colors. Flowers were beginning to bloom and the aftermath of the last spring snowstorm was still present. Street erosion from the salt trucks was tearing cars up like the city was on the mechanics' pay role.

Butta met TE` for lunch at a private café. They had been kicking it since a few weeks prior when TE` took her home and waxed that ass. TE` was not in denial. He knew Evea was really who he wanted; but he was just having fun with Butta for the moment. Butta did not mind. She was used to being a second string bench rider. At the rate they were going she just thought that she just might be moved to a starting position. She figured if she keeps eating his gun up like a pro he would get sprung. Little did she know Evea could eat a gun up in her sleep and separate cum from the condom. So Butta was no competition.

TE` and Butta sat there enjoying the first day of spring. The weather felt more like mid-summer. People were out and about. Females were half dressed, showing off their new spring gear. Butta was talking about everything under the sun while TE` just sat there and stared into space. TE` looked at Butta really good and began to feel like he was being taken for a ride. He began to feel sick to his stomach. He could not even finish his T-bone steak-and-egg platter. Butta was so busy talking that she did not notice the change in his mood.

As TE` stared at her, he was reminded of his two cousins Chae and Diamond. They were gorgeous and every nigga in the hood wanted to get at them. They never paid for anything and always had money. They both stayed in the latest Reeboks and Guess jeans when they were growing up, and their jewelry was big and flashy. Chae had some earrings the size of a small child's face. They were tricking since the young age of fourteen. TE` new how scandalous bitches could be and he had started to see Butta for who she was. His cousins taught him a lot of things about how fucked up females could have any nigga from thugs to corporate white collars. Chae and Diamond did whatever they had to do while fucking and sucking for money and status. The sad part was that they never thought about what they were doing as whoring or tricking.

TE` began to come out of his trance when he heard several motorcycles blaze by. The street appeared as if it was littered with Jolly-Rancher candy. There were bikes of all different colors blazing through the bright sunny street. TE`s eyes grew wide. He said, "Damn!" out loud, before he even realized it. He was drawn to the only female rider in the crew. She was thick and juicy like a well-prepared steak. Her beautiful curves even showed while she sat on her fully tricked out silver, hot pink and black 1000 Yamaha. Her ass spilled over the seat and vibrated with every rev of the motor.

"TE`! TE`!" Butta called out, and broke TE' out of his trance. "I know you are not going to check some other girl out in my face!"

TE` just stared at her and said with no regard, "Are you finished yet? I got to go handle some business."

A bit shocked at his indifference, she nodded her head and TE` gestured for the waiter.

The ride home was silent as Jamie Foxx sang on the radio; "DJ won't you play this girl a love song, cause she really needs to hear a freaking love song ……….she needs me to beat it beat it!"

Butta could feel the tension and she was confused about where it came from. She felt TE` slowly drifting away. TE` turned down a street filled with trees and pretty budding flowers in hues of vivid purples and pinks. Butta seized the moment and began to massage his crotch. TE` began to moan and soon the car road a little slower. Butta bent over and buried her head in his lap. She gave up knowledge like a college professor. Her head moved up down and around methodically to the beat of the song. TE` could not stand it anymore. He pulled over on the side of the road. Cars behind him beeped as they went pass. The thought that people were watching them turned her on even more. She climbed over the seat and sat on TE`s lap with her back facing him. She rocked back and forth, not letting his dick get a break. She was enjoying the ride. Her clit rubbed up against his gray Polo khakis.

Soon she began to jerk and moan in the sexiest cum voice TE` had ever heard. TE`s pants were stained with sweet pussy juices. She got up and went back to her business. She inhaled his dick like she had asthma and his dick was a rescue pump. TE`s entire body shook, "OOOOOOOOOOH, SHIIIIIIIT!" He screamed as Butta ushered his DNA down her throat. TE` looked down in amazement and BUTTA looked up at him with her pretty seductive eyes. She softly whispered to him, "Welcome back, baby."

A tap at the door and a ring on his cell phone alerted Zayne that Naih had arrived. He was ready and waiting for her beautiful Goddess like stature to be revealed. Zayne, being as cautious as he was, still toted his gun. The door swung open and Zayne was a sight for sore eyes. There he stood buck-naked holding two guns! Naih had plans of using one of them.

She entered the house and they attacked each other like wild, vicious animals.

Zayne wanted to fuck. He was in a straight-to-the-point mood. He pulled her close to him and spun her around to the back. Zayne bit her back and her neck as her moans filled the air like sweet aroma. Zayne led her over to a soft leather couch in the center of the living room. Before Naih could get any words out she was bent over and her denim Apple Bottom skirt was hiked up around her small waist. Naih's long jet-black hair hung over the cream sofa. Zayne was in full brick mode. His chocolate rod was ready for pleasure. He admired her wide, substantial ass as he stood behind her preparing to dive deep into her sea. The anticipation almost killed Naih. She begged him to stick it in. Her pussy walls cried out to be filled up with his essence. Zayne finished putting on his ultra-sensitive Magnum. Naih looked over her right shoulder to give him the hurry up look. Just at that moment when their eyes met, Zayne plunged in so deep that Naih could not react, all she could do is moan low and slowly, "Mmmmmmm…." She moaned, satisfied at last.

They were finally finished with round one; they lay in each other's arms talking business. Zayne questioned her about what she had to tell him. Naih explained that she overheard Noah on the phone talking about Manny and he mention the name Adam and named him as his connect. She also told him that he was scheduled to meet him at pier 11 at the upcoming Spring Fling on Delaware Avenue. Zayne confirmed this information with her. He said to Naih, "I knew it was something about that guy I did not like. I want you to make sure you go with Noah to the pier and I will already be there waiting for them niggas. I don't want that nigga to start suspecting that you are dirty!"

"What if he don't ask me to go?" Naih questioned. Zayne instructed her to call him and ask him if he does not call her. Spring Fling was a big event in Philly to kick off spring fever; everybody that was anybody would be there.

Ring, Ring, Ring!

"Yo, what's up nigga?"

"Nothing, what's up with you?" TE' replied.

"I was calling to make sure everything was set."

"Yeah, yeah, everything is cool."

"That bitch has not called me yet. I wonder if she took the bait?" Noah asked.

"Stop bitching. She will contact you. And I know she is a faithful bitch to her niggas anytime she fucked your ass for information! Trust me, she told them everything she heard. Just don't forget pier 11."

"TE`, how are we going to get that pretty muthafuka there?"

"He got a note from Evea- or should I say he thinks the note is from her- trust me, he will be there."

Beep, beep, beep.

"Yo, I'll holla at you, that is my other line." Noah clicked over, and to his surprise it was Naih calling to invite him to the Spring Fling. Noah agreed and everything was set. He could not wait to get Naih back for trying to play him and Adam. But paybacks sometimes charged interest.

Chapter 15

GRAND FINALE

"Hello," Evea called Tiff.

"What's up young girl? What are you into right now, or should I say, what are you trying to get into?" Evea said sarcastically.

Tiff gathered her thoughts and told Evea that she was asleep before she called. Evea was excited about Spring Fling and she wanted Tiff and Lex to go with her and TE` on a double date. Tiff knew this could never happen since she figured out that Lex was the one who shot Evea. Tiff was determined to find out Lex and Adam's connection.

"Tiff, I said what are you getting into? I want to know because I want you and Lex to go to the Spring Fling with us," Evea reiterated.

"Bitch, what you think this is? You know I don't do the double date thing!" Tiff replied with an attitude. "I don't want that nigga to know none of my peoples. I might have to slump that nigga one day!" Evea cracked up laughing at Tiff. Little did she know Tiff was planning to fuck Lex one last time and slump his ass for real.

"So, what you saying… You not going to Spring Fling? I know that is a lie!"

"No, bitch, pay attention! I'm telling you that I am not going with you and TE`! Now if we were ditching the niggas…. I would role with you!"

"You know I can't…"

"Evea, hold it, just save the drama. What you can do is go with me to get my Fuck-His-Head-Up outfit."

Evea knew she was not going to change Tiff's mind so she said, "Ok, I will meet you at the mall."

Tiff hung up with Evea and realized the harsh reality: she was going to be saying good-bye to Lex no matter what.

"What's up nigga?" a scratchy voice came through the receiver.

"Nothing," Corn replied. "I got this. I have everything prepared. I already spoke to Jay-Rock and Love and they are well informed of their

roles in this situation. We will be there an hour before you and in place."

"Okay nigga, I know you got me."

TE` knew he could count on Corn and all his close-knit niggas. They were all like brothers and definitely RIDERS. TE` hung up with Corn and went to pick up his outfit for the evening. Corn went to New York to get his outfit; he had to look good even handling business. Jay-Rock and Love went to a local designer to lay them out just right. They knew that it would be plenty of bitches at Spring Fling and they were planning on getting a few of them before and after handling their business. Jay-Roc was excited; he could not wait to give Adam what he deserved, and the other niggas that tried to get at TE' their helping to.

Evea arrived home two hours before her and TE` was to leave for the Spring Fling. She wanted to be on time to see the start of the fashion show. She noticed that TE` had already picked up his outfit and left it on the bed. She went through the house calling him, trying to figure out where he was. "TE`! TE`!" she yelled. She found TE` in the basement cleaning three guns. He had a chrome 9mm special with hallow bullets, a 45 revolver and a mini 380 that fit in the small of his back. Evea stood there for a minute, then said: "What the fuck are you doing!?"

TE` turned around so fast that he dropped his gun, his eyes appeared to be marbles. "Why are you spying on me?"

After a moment of surprised guilt, TE' tried to regain control of the conversation: "I have these guns for your protection. You know there be millions at Spring Fling; I have to be prepared."

Evea gave him a look as if to say she was watching him. "Damn! You don't need three guns for that!"

"Girl. I'm a grown ass man. Don't start your shit. Just go get dressed."

Evea was shocked. She turned around and marched back to their bedroom. She was pissed, but it was true that TE`s stern demeanor turned Evea on. Suddenly she heard her cell phone alert her that she had missed a call. It was Adam. She put the code in her phone that meant 'see you later.' Evea thought to herself that she could not meet him later, and she hoped he was not going to try to see her at Spring Fling.

Tiff danced around her house singing to Destiny's Child's old Destiny Fulfilled CD. She laid her clothes out and began her beauty ritual. She had to meet Lex at Spring Fling. Tiff prepared her all black 380 to be toted like a brand new Gucci bag. Tiff placed her thigh holster on and made sure that her gun was on safety, and then she put the gun in its place. Tiff was dressed in all black Armani linen. She wore a mini skirt with a linen jeweled halter-top and a bright yellow oversized Gucci bag. She looked at her reflection in the mirror and gave a big smile as she shook her ass; then she headed for the door.

Corn and the fellas arrived in style. They all rode with Corn in one of his latest attention-getters. He pulled up to the gala in a money green 2007 Bentley, fresh off the showroom floor. He always copped the upcoming year's ride around springtime. The car was equipped with 24 inch rims that kept spinning as they blinded onlookers. The interior was tricked out with televisions and all the latest gadgets. The sand color butter leather reclaimed its form as all of the fellas got out of the car. Females stood around creaming in their panties as they each exited the vehicle. Corn adorned his perfectly sculpted body with a soft green, handmade Egyptian silk and linen Capri set. He wore camel color Kenneth Cole sandals, and he was blinging from neck to fingers. Jay-Rock played a red and black linen outfit with black Armani slide-ins. Love was chocolate and he knew just what colors complimented his complexion. He was styling in a soft yellow linen pants suit with chocolate brown, square-toe Gavelli sandals. They were all fresh to death. Corn and the guys mingled a little with some females and then they made their way to the pier.

Evea and TE` arrived a short while later. The stage and the atmosphere were electric. The energy of beautiful weather and beautiful people were in the air. TE` and Evea fit right into the denim and linen theme of the evening. TE` wore a gray and pink linen and denim outfit. He wore butter soft salmon-pink Gucci sandals. Evea complimented him with a pink linen one-piece dress with crisscross straps and a linen and denim mini jacket. She wore a pair of Dolce & Gabbana open toe jeweled 3-inch heels. The stage was decorated with crystals and roses. The jewels on the stage glittered as the models strutted down the runway in the latest spring and summer fashions by all of the top designers. TE` was getting restless. He knew that the fashion show was almost over and the concert was going to be starting soon. He knew that was when he would make his move.

Adam arrived at the Spring Fling a little late and he made his way through the crowd. He was on his way to the pier to meet Evea. He was held up by security. He was told he had to wait a few more minutes until they were letting anyone else past the ropes. Adam stood there impatiently. He could not wait to be in his lover's presence one more time.

Tiff arrived at the show and was searching for Lex. While she was looking the opposite way, Lex crept up behind her dressed in white linen. Lex grabbed her waist and said, "Damn Ma, you sexy as shit. Aare you waiting for someone?" He loved to creep up on her; that was his style.

Tiff poked her ass out and replied, "I think I just found him!" They both laughed.

Tiff was falling harder than she thought, which made her task even harder to complete. Tiff loved fucking Lex and she was determined to follow through with the first half of her plan. Tiff self-parked in the parking lot to make sure she would be able to taste that dick once more. Tiff told Lex that she left something in her car and needed his assistance to walk back and get it. Lex found it odd that Tiff did not use valet parking; but he followed her anyway.

While Tiff was on her way to get her last shot, Naih and Noah arrived at the party. They wore all-white denim. Noah and Naih sat a few rows back from TE` and Evea. Naih was nervous, but she was packing heat so she had protection. She was trying to figure out how she would get away to get to pier 11 before Noah. Noah could not wait to give her what he thought she deserved.

Tiff and Lex made it to the car and Tiff bent over pretending to look for her purse. Lex saw that she had no panties on.

"Damn Ma, you got a nigga on brick!"

Lex's hormones rode hard like wild stallions. Tiff forgot that she had her gun on her right thigh. Lex saw how the black holster and gun rested on her toned thigh. This made him more aroused. Tiff knew this turned him on so she hiked her ass up more and made sure she had a perfect arch in her back. Lex moved closer to Tiff and began to put his fingers in her wet ocean. She was so wet that her pussy talked back to him like it had vocal cords. Tiff climbed in the car and spread her legs open as she invited Lex in for dinner. Lex dove in headfirst and licked from front to back until Tiff's seats were drenched with lust.

The security guard allowed Adam through. It was intermission and the fashion show was over. The music was about to begin as Adam slowly moved through the crowd and said 'excuse me' to the hundreds of people in the walkway. The Spring Fling show was packed due to the big names on the docket. Beyonce` and Jay-Z, TI, Little Wayne and Chris Brown- just to name a few of the scheduled performances. Adam was almost past the stage and he could see a clear walkway. Lex and Tiff had just arrived at the seating area. They had a great time in the car and Tiff was glowing brighter than the jewels on the stage. They walked up, trying to be seated, laughing about their brief episode. Lex noticed a tall, curly head nigga fighting to get through the crowd ahead of him. He thought to himself, "That can't be Adam." Adam turned sideways to let someone get past and Lex confirmed it. He had to follow him and finish what he had started. He thought quickly what he was going to say to Tiff to get away. They made it to their seats and Lex stood up and told Tiff, "Yo Ma, I'll be back. I just saw one of my homeys- I am going to go holla at him."

Tiff looked at him and noticed that he had begun to sweat. She said to herself, "Okay, homey my ass." Tiff was determined to let Lex go handle his business.

The lights started flashing and TI hit the stage, "What You Know About That," sounded over the speakers; the crowd went wild. TE` told Evea that he was going to the bathroom. Noah got up and began to move when he saw TE` get up. Naih had left about ten minutes prior to the show starting. She told Noah she had to go to the restroom. She was on her way to meet Zayne at the pier.

Adam got through the crowd and made it to pier 11 and no one was there. He stood there looking at his watch and anticipating another brief moment with his love. Corn and the rest of the crew were in the building right above the pier with their weapons drawn and pointed at the center of the pier. Zayne and Naih were in position behind two old dumpsters like two children playing a game of hide and seek. They could not wait to see Noah so Zayne could make his move. Adam turned around and looked at the water reminiscing about Evea and his last time together. Lex quickly appeared with gun drawn. Adam heard a heavier foot than a female and at that moment he realized he was set up. He spun around with his gun drawn. Both men stood there with their guns pointed at each other. Adam was confused he did not know Lex and did not know what he wanted with him. Adam stood there with a Chrome Desert Eagle pointed in his face, "Who the fuck are you?"

"Nigga, I'm your worse nightmare!" Lex said. "I should have finished you off in your car… this time I won't miss!"

"Pussy, you are the one that shot my baby…" Adam said, looking Lex straight in the eye.

Lex let off a shot that hit Adam so hard he stumbled backward. Adam returned fire and hit Lex in the stomach. Corn and the boys witnessed the shit go down. Corn told them to hold their fire because Lex was down there. Corn did not know how Lex knew

Adam and he could not make out what they were saying to each other.

Zayne emerged from behind the huge dumpster. He walked up behind Adam and said, "You dirty nigga, drop the fucking gun!"

Naih ran from under the overpass yelling, "That's not Noah! Wait!"

She startled them and shots rang out. Naih fell to the ground. Her blood turned the cement a deep burgundy hue. Adam was shot in the chest but he managed to run for cover as bullets flew from everywhere. He made it a few feet away then collapse on his stomach. TE` and Noah arrived just in time. They walked up, letting bullets rain down like spring showers. Zayne managed to maneuver his way behind a cement bolder.

The last conversation he had with Evea ran through Adam's mind; he accepted that he might not make it through the shootout alive. Zayne was on wild-out mode. He didn't give a fuck. His love was shot and possibly dead. He was out to revenge his homey's death.

Lex was hurt, alone and he had several niggas shooting at him. He saw vision of many faces of the niggas that he killed throughout his years of being the crew's enforcer. He did not know how TE` and Noah were involved with the situation, but he did not care. The only thing on his mind was surviving; so he busted shots at them too.

Tiff began to worry and she got up to go look for Lex. She got a few blocks away from the show and heard shots. She quickly took her gun from her holster. She walked up and saw Lex being shot at. She could not see who was shooting. Tiff wanted to walk away and let the niggas shooting at him do her dirty work. Lex stood up to return a shot and was shot several times in the torso. He fell to the ground, gasping for air. Tiff stopped dead in her tracks screaming, "NOOOOOOOO!" She ran up dumping back; she hit Zayne in the head and he fell to the ground lifeless. At that moment, she knew she was in too deep to just walk away.

TE ` was still after blood! Adam body lay on the ground still and TE` could not express the rage he felt for him in words, instead he allowed his gat to speak for him. TE` stood over Adams motionless body and reloaded his clip. When TE`s clip locked into place Adam rolled over with blood stained eyes piercing through TE letting his gun ring like a four alarm fire alert.

He said,

"Your wife was a great fuck! But now I'm going to fuck you up!" His words were harsh and reeked of rage and detest.

Tiff crawled low and pulled Lex to safety. Her lover, who just a few hours ago she planned to murder, was now her priority. She struggled with mixed emotions. She held him in her arms and he spoke the three words they had never spoken to each other.

"MA, I 'm not going to make it. I can feel it."

Tiff begged him not to say that.

"Listen, I'm fucked up bad MA! I love you…I loved you from the first day we…" Lex's breath evaporated like steam from a boiling teapot. Tiff was on her knees weeping. For the first time, she found love, and she couldn't even keep it. She kneeled there with sounds of bullets echoing in the background as her heart turned to stone.

Her tears covered Lex, but they were not enough to save him. His lifeless body lay in her arms. Bullets and bodies surrounded Tiff. She struggle to process everything that had just taken place. Tiff continued to weep uncontrollably over Lex's corpse. She gathered her gun and some of Lex's personal belongings and anything else that she deemed important. She headed back toward the show with a slow lurch. She was fucked up over the shit that had just went down; but she was still a wise gangstress. She knew that the police would soon be arriving on the scene and she needed to be far away. Tiff walked back for blocks replaying what she had witnessed and had been involved in her head and wondering how she would go on. She got one block from the show and tried to pull herself together before she saw Evea. Tiff stood startled by Evea's abrupt appearance. Evea was on her way to see what was taking TE` so long at the bathroom. She looked as if she saw a ghost floating in mid air. Evea did not say a word her face had a vocabulary of its own. Tiff stood there with TE`s bloody shirt in her hand, Lex's chain, car keys and gun in the other. Evea approached Tiff with caution and took the gun out of her right hand. Tiff fell to the ground taking Evea with her as she let out cries of screeching wild animals in pain. Evea wrapped her up in her arms matching Tiff's screams.

Deep beneath their consoling embrace festered turmoil and hatred.

A Sneak Peek of

INSIDE OUT 360

INTRODUCTION

The streets were lined with beautiful trees. Hues of yellow and powder blue surrounded each branch. The sweet smell of floral essence floated through the air and made it known that spring was fast approaching. The busy streets where cars rode to and fro sat smack in the center of Philadelphia's posh neighborhood Balla Cynwood. The home of ballers, city's top officials and a few well known street pharmacist. The tall buildings surrounding the area were the work places of some of the most influential doctors and lawyers.

Tiff pulled up to the front of a twenty story plush building. She checked herself in her rear view mirror and proceeded to exit her car. She turned around to set the alarm on her latest toy, a sea-blue Benz convertible.

Cars slowed down as she strutted across the parking lot dressed in a one piece strapless denim jumper and 2 inch studded Marc Jacob's stilettos. Her hair was a flowing mane of layers and her Chanel Shades were perfect for her small face. Tiff was on a mission and even though she felt like crap she definitely didn't look like it. She lived by her motto "Never Let em See you Sweat".

Tiff was on her way to her standing appointment with Dr. Deborah Hawkins every other week since six weeks ago. She was feeling so bad on many levels. She and Evea were not in touch with each other in years and the love of her life death anniversary was slowly approaching.

Tiff stepped off of the elevator and was greeted by Dr. Hawkins secretary who always was pleasant and made her feel comfortable.

Good morning Ms. Dease I'm glad to see you made it in. Tiff gave a half smile and replied, "yeah I almost turned around at least 5 times on my way over here."

"Well you know Dr. Hawkins would have hunted you down."

Both ladies laughed at the thought Dr. Hawkins running in her good heals to catch Tiff. As the ladies finished their good laugh the Dr. appeared in her doorway to usher Tiff into her office.

Dr. Hawkins stood 5ft 7 inch, with natural curly shoulder length hair and milk chocolate skin. "Hello Ms. Tiffany I'm glad to see you smiling these days."

Tiff replied, "not for long." The office was decorated in calm colors, cream and sea-foam green. The doctor escorted Tiff in and directed her to lay on her comfortable Chase that sat in the left corner of the room in front of the window. Tiff obliged her as she lay steering at the selling. Tears began to stream down her face at the thought of re-living that horrible night when her love was taken from her. Tiff blamed Evea for everything. Rapid thoughts raced through her mind as she talked to herself "Evea why did you have to be so selfish, now I lost you and Lex. Dr. Hawkins gathered up some tissues and handed them to Tiff.

"Tiffany why are you crying?"

Tiff just sobbed even more. The Doctor explained that if she was not ready to face that night they could reschedule the hypnoses session. Tiff sniffed and replied "Doc I'm ready to put this behind me let's do this."

Dr. Hawkins began relaxing Tiff and asking her a series of questions to take her back to where all of her pain began.

Tiff grabbed hold of the pillow and ushered Dr. Hawkins into her world.

Tiff arrived at the show and was searching for Lex. While she was looking the opposite way, Lex crept up behind her dressed in white linen. Lex grabbed her waist and said, "Damn Ma, you sexy as shit. Are you waiting for someone?" He loved to creep up on her; that was his style.

Tiff poked her ass out and replied, "I think I just found him!" They both laughed.

Tiff was falling harder than she thought, which made her task even harder to complete. Tiff loved fucking Lex and she was determined to follow through with the first half of her plan. Tiff self-parked in the parking lot to make sure she would be able to taste that dick once more. Tiff told Lex that she left something in her car and needed his assistance to walk back and get it. Lex found it odd that Tiff did not use valet parking; but he followed her anyway.

While Tiff was on her way to get her last shot, Naih and Noah arrived at the party. They wore all-white denim. Noah and Naih sat a few rows back from TE` and Evea. Naih was *nervous, but she was packing heat so she had protection. She was trying to figure out how she would get away to get to pier 11 before Noah. Noah could not wait to give her what he thought she deserved.*

Tiff and Lex made it to the car and Tiff bent over pretending to look for her purse. Lex saw that she had no panties on.

"Damn Ma, you got a nigga on brick!"

Lex's hormones rode hard like wild stallions. Tiff forgot that she had her gun on her right thigh. Lex saw how the black holster and gun rested on her toned thigh. This made him more aroused. Tiff knew this turned him on so she hiked her ass up more and made sure she had a perfect arch in her back. Lex moved closer to Tiff and began to put his fingers in her wet ocean. She was so wet that her pussy talked back to him like it had vocal cords. Tiff climbed in the car and spread her legs open as she invited Lex in for dinner. Lex dove in headfirst and licked from front to back until Tiff's seats were drenched with lust.

The security guard allowed Adam through. It was intermission and the fashion show was over. The music was about to begin as Adam slowly moved through the crowd and said 'excuse me' to the hundreds of people in the walkway. The Spring Fling show was packed due to the big names on the docket. Beyonce` and Jay-Z, TI, Little Wayne and Chris Brown- just to name a few of the scheduled performances. Adam was almost past the stage and he could see a clear walkway. Lex and Tiff had *just arrived at the seating area. They had a great time in the car and Tiff was glowing brighter than the jewels on the stage. They walked up, trying to be seated, laughing about their brief episode. Lex noticed a tall, curly head nigga fighting to get through the crowd ahead of him. He thought to himself, "That can't be Adam." Adam turned sideways to let someone get past and Lex confirmed it. He had to follow him and finish what he had started. He thought quickly what he was going to say to Tiff to get away. They made it to their seats and Lex stood up and told Tiff, "Yo Ma, I'll be back. I just saw one of my homeys- I am going to go holla at him."*

Tiff looked at him and noticed that he had begun to sweat. She said to herself, "Okay, homey my ass." Tiff was determined to let Lex go handle his business.

The lights started flashing and TI hit the stage, "What You Know About That," sounded over the speakers; the crowd went wild. TE` told Evea that he was going to the bathroom. Noah got up and began to move when he saw TE` get up. Naih had left about ten minutes prior to the show starting. She told Noah she had to go to the restroom. She was on her way to meet Zayne at the pier.

Adam got through the crowd and made it to pier 11 and no one was there. He stood there looking at his watch and anticipating another brief moment with his love. Corn and the rest of the crew were in the building right above the pier with their weapons drawn and pointed at the center of the pier. Zayne and Naih were in position behind two old dumpsters like two children playing a game of hide and seek. They could not wait to see Noah so Zayne could make his move. Adam turned around and looked at the water reminiscing about Evea and his last time together. Lex quickly appeared with gun drawn. Adam heard a heavier foot than a female and at that moment he realized he was set up. He spun around with his gun drawn. Both men stood there with their guns pointed at each other. Adam was confused he did not know Lex and did not know what he wanted with him. Adam stood there with a Chrome Desert Eagle pointed in his face, "Who the fuck are you?"

"Nigga, I'm your worse nightmare!" Lex said. "I should have finished you off in your car… this time I won't miss!"

"Pussy, you are the one that shot my baby…" Adam said, looking Lex straight in the eye.

Lex let off a shot that hit Adam so hard he stumbled backward. Adam returned fire and hit Lex in the stomach. Corn and the boys witnessed the shit go down. Corn told them to hold their fire because Lex was down there. Corn did not know how Lex knew Adam and he could not make out what they were saying to each other.

Zayne emerged from behind the huge dumpster. He walked up behind Adam and said, "You dirty nigga, drop the fucking gun!"

Naih ran from under the overpass yelling, "That's not Noah! Wait!"

She startled them and shots rang out. Naih fell to the ground. Her blood turned the cement a deep burgundy hue. Adam was shot in the chest but he managed to run for cover as bullets flew from everywhere. He made it a few feet away then collapse on his stomach. TE` and Noah arrived just in time. They walked up, letting bullets rain down like spring showers. Zayne managed to maneuver his way behind a cement bolder.

The last conversation he had with Evea ran through Adam's mind; he accepted that he might not make it through the shootout alive. Zayne was on wild-out mode. He didn't give a fuck. His love was shot and possibly dead. He was out to revenge his homey's death.

Lex was hurt, alone and he had several niggas shooting at him. He saw vision of many faces of the niggas that he killed throughout his years of being the crew's enforcer. He did not know how TE` and Noah were involved with the situation, but he did not care. The only thing on his mind was surviving; so he busted shots at them too.

Tiff began to worry and she got up to go look for Lex. She got a few blocks away from the show and heard shots. She quickly took her gun from her holster. She walked up and saw Lex being shot at. She could not see who was shooting. Tiff wanted to walk away and let the niggas shooting at him do her dirty work. Lex stood up to return a shot and was shot several times in the torso. He fell to the ground, gasping for air. Tiff stopped dead in her tracks screaming, "NOOOOOOOO!" She ran up dumping back; she hit Zayne in the head and he fell to the ground lifeless. At that moment, she knew she was in too deep to just walk away.

TE ` was still after blood! Adam body lay on the ground still and TE` could not express the rage he felt for him in words, instead he allowed his gat to speak for him. TE` stood over Adams motionless body and reloaded his clip. When TE`s clip locked into place Adam rolled over with blood stained eyes piercing through TE letting his gun ring like a four alarm fire alert.

He said,

"Your wife was a great fuck! But now I'm going to fuck you up!" His words were harsh and reeked of rage and detest.

Tiff crawled low and pulled Lex to safety. Her lover, who just a few hours ago she planned to murder, was now her priority. She struggled with mixed emotions. She held him in her arms and he spoke the three words they had never spoken to each other.

"MA, I 'm not going to make it. I can feel it."

Tiff begged him not to say that.

"Listen, I'm fucked up bad MA! I love you…I loved you from the first day we…" Lex's breath evaporated like steam

from a boiling teapot. Tiff was on her knees weeping. For the first time, she found love, and she couldn't even keep it. She kneeled there with sounds of bullets echoing in the background as her heart turned to stone.

Her tears covered Lex, but they were not enough to save him. His lifeless body lay in her arms. Bullets and bodies surrounded Tiff. She struggle to process everything that had just taken place. Tiff continued to weep uncontrollably over Lex's corpse. She gathered her gun and some of Lex's personal belongings and anything else that she deemed important. She headed back toward the show with a slow lurch. She was fucked up over the shit that had just went down; but she was still a wise gangstress. She knew that the police would soon be arriving on the scene and she needed to be far away. Tiff walked back for blocks replaying what she had witnessed and had been involved in her head and wondering how she would go on. She got one block from the show and tried to pull herself together before she saw Evea. Tiff stood startled by Evea's abrupt appearance. Evea was on her way to see what was taking TE` so long at the bathroom. She looked as if she saw a ghost floating in mid air. Evea did not say a word her face had a vocabulary of its own. Tiff stood there with TE`s bloody shirt in her hand, Lex's chain, car keys and gun in the other. Evea approached Tiff with caution and took the gun out of her right hand. Tiff fell to the ground taking Evea with her as she let out cries of screeching wild animals in pain. Evea wrapped her up in *her arms matching Tiff's screams. Deep beneath their consoling embrace festered turmoil and hatred.*

CHAPTER 1

"Yo where that cash at nigga!"

" I told you I would have it later on today"

"You said that shit two days ago!"

The angry gunman pulled out his nine cocked back and let off a round. Noah dodged and ran as he gave the gunman some of his own hot shit back. Noah's luck ran out and all he saw last was the smoke from the barrel…

"Keep the change Nigga!"

Bang, bang! The banging on the door woke Noah up from his nightmare. He jumped out of bed sweating and breathing like he had just run 10 miles straight. "Who is it!" he yelled angrier that he just got mirked in his dream than that the door woke him up. "It's me Corn nigga what's taking ya ass so long?"

Noah made it to the door and swung it open when he heard the familiar voice on the other end. Corn entered the house and walked slowly down Noah's long hallway where the floors were Italian- marble and the pictures on the wall were fine art fresh out of the art gallery. Corn questioned Noah, "Why you not ready we was supposed to meet the fellas at the spot 30 minutes ago."

"Man I was having this crazy ass dream I had to lay a nigga down in this one"

Corn laughed and replied, "Nigga how you sweating and breathing look like a nigga laid your ass down in your dream." Noah stopped and just looked at Corn hating the fact that he was on the right track. " I'll be ready in a minute call the crew and let them know we on our way. Corn said, "Cool just hurry up man, this shit never happened when TE` was here."

"Nigga please."

Noah ran up stairs to go shower and get fresh for their business meeting. Since TE` was gone Noah had been running shit and he was finding out that being the head nigga in charged was harder than he thought. Noah emerged from his bedroom suite looking duggy. His curly dark black dreads were lying perfectly in place and his shape up was tight. He had on black denim Cavelli Jeans and a jeweled out Ed Hardy tee shirt. Noah was toting his accessory that matched everything; his nickel-plated nine equipped with silencer. He was ready for whatever and willing to ride or die.

Noah hurried down the stairs so Corn would not be any more restless than usual. "My nigga what's the deal?" Noah yelled to let Corn know he was ready to go. Corn held up his right index finger to signal Noah to be quiet while he was finishing up his call.

"Damn nigga who you speaking on the phone with that important that I got to get the church finger?"

Corn shot back, "Now you worried about the wrong shit my nig"

They both gave each other some dap and headed out the door. Corn and Noah walked down the wide long driveway trying to decide which hot ride they would take, one of Noah's or Corn's brand new dopeboy slick black Range Rover. They jumped in Corn's ride and proceeded to their destination. On the ride over to the west Philly spot they discussed crew shit and the latest territory they were trying to take over. Corn loved Noah like a brother but it was obvious that he was not TE`. Noah was wild and at times reckless in his business decisions. That was one of the reasons that TE` kept him as the sniper. He was ready to let off whenever. Noah gambled too much and did plenty of fucking, which was always his weakness. He was part of the reason the girl Naih was able to infiltrate and try to set TE` and the crew up at the shoot out.

They arrived at the spot. The block was jumping. Fiends were everywhere and the little homies were serving heavy. That was a sign of great business and profit to come. Noah and Corn hopped out of the Range and proceeded to walk up the block. Bitches stopped and waived as they creamed in their panties at the sight of fresh money and power. The sun was shining bright and everyone was buzzing about the upcoming spring fling in the city. The small-overcrowded street was filled with row homes where every other house was boarded up. Corn and Noah said what's up to the homies as they walked through like celebrities. They reached their destination and the street soldiers on the porch were on point and load with heavy firepower. They each gave dap as they approached the front door of the army green painted house. They did the special knock to be sure the boys inside didn't let off shots when they opened the door. They entered the spot and it was what up my niggas all around the room. Jay-Roc was at the table ready for the business meeting. Love was on his cell phone boo-lovin with his latest booty call, which is how he got his name in the first place and G was sitting on the brown leather sofa playing Madden. Noah eyes canvassed the room and stopped dead on the new comer. G turned around and Noah looked as if he saw a ghost… "What's up my nigga!!!! When did you get home"

Noah was so happy to see one of the old crewmembers finally out of the pin. G did some hard time for TE` back in the day and was just hitting the streets. "I just touched down last night nigga , I see you still the same old Noah Just a little older than I remember."

Both men embraced as they shared a mutual laugh about Noah's habit of going against the grain. Love, by this time had hung up the phone and chimed in, "nigga that's why we had the meeting set with such short notice it was supposed to be a surprise and instead you surprised us by taking all damn day, fake ass pretty boy. U ain't even light-skin" They all roared in laughter. "Alright, that's enough of that Noah yelled out as to appear to be serious now."

Jay-Roc yelled out, "Go to Hell" The men slowly got themselves together and made their way to the table. Noah took TE`s seat at the head of the table. It still felt funny to be sitting in his deceased cousin's spot. Noah and TE` were very close and he took his death harder than any one of them. He felt even more fucked up that day because looking at G was like looking at TE`. They were always told that they looked alike when they were growing up. G stood about 6ft 3 and was light brown, with dark wavy hair and a full rich beard. The only thing that separated TE` and G was the hair on G's head. The meeting went on.

Corn began by informing the boys that the block was doing wonderful bringing in like 50,000 every few days per house. The fellas all were yelling and cheering for the success of their empire. G just sat there thinking "damn my homies are really eating and I'm about to get a piece of the pie too." G was anxious to discuss the most anticipated topic of the hour. He interrupted the buzz, "Yo I know we celebrating me coming home and our shit bombing; but I need to know something, did this nigga Adam get touched yet for offing my big homie TE`?" The mention of his name choked G up and brought him to rage all at the same time. Noah replied, "That nigga done went into hiding for some years since this shit went down and nobody have seen him I mean nobody"

"What happened to Evea?"

"She been missing too, Kayla is with Evea's mother and nobody really knows where that is" Evea was real fucked up after TE`s death.

G just sat there staring into space. Kayla was his goddaughter and he had missed so much of her life, now his one true friend was gone and he may never see Kayla again.

"Kayla has to be about 15 or 16 years old now right"

Noah counted the years on his fingers then looked up and said "yeah that's about right".

G excused himself from the table and went outside for some air. The fellas resumed their meeting without commenting on G's obvious mood. Corn asked, "Okay next order of business is G's coming home party. Did you book the usual place and is everything ready?" Jay-

Roc replied, "yes-sir everything is in place I'm ready for some get right tonight!"

Noah sat back in the chair and looked around the room as if he was expecting five-o to rush in any minute. "We need to wrap this shit up, what's going on with the new spot we are opening?"

Love replied, "I'm on that right now. I was just talking to my connect when you came in. She put me on to this little town in upstate PA that don't have nobody else supplying all of the rich white folks wit that pure nose candy." Noah got a little more comfortable in his chair. Love continued, " If everything works out we will be making double what we making at the other houses weekly."

Everybody said, "Damn" all at once like a church choir.

Love went on, me and honey gone rent a place as a couple in fake names and take over the Burbs, Mr. And Mrs. Snowman"

Noah said "that sounds good but I don't know this chic how you know she clean?"

"Cause I know, trust me she won't be involved in any day to day operations.

Noah's Phone rang and broke up the party. "Yo talk to me sexy"

“Hey baby where you at” a sultry voice said through the phone.

“I’m finishing up with the boys why what’s good”

“That good dick, that’s what’s good, and me sliding down on it!”

“Damn Shawty you got a nigga on brick, hold on”

Corn said, “We know meeting over” they all got up from the table as they cracked up in laughter.

Jay yelled, “That must be Ms. Boss Bitch”

Noah fanned him away with his hand.

Noah returned to the phone, “Shawty I’m on my way!”

Noah rushed out of the door and gave all the fellas some dap on the way to the car. He said his good you home to G and headed for the Range. Corn knew what he was up to so he did not even ask. Corn just threw him the keys and told Noah he would meet up with him later at the party. Noah turned around and yelled back, “Be sure to take care of G”

G laughed and looked at Corn, “Still the same old Noah, slave to the pussy.”

Corn replied, “I'll say yes master to some good pussy any day!” Noah hit the e-way like a bat out of hell he was ready to experience all his shawty had to give. He could not control the erection he got just thinking about her. How sexy she was and the shit she did to him was something out of a book or movie. He was ready to be taken to the edge and hung off the cliff. Noah loved all the things that got his adrenaline going like great sex, money and gambling all in that order. Noah hit full speed ahead and put Corn's system to use. He blasted plies all the way home as he nodded his head and sang along with each verse. He could see the house in his view and was growing more excited as he exited the e-way. Noah pulled up to the huge driveway and noticed his Shawty's car was already there. So that could mean only one thing she was inside thinking and preparing for their encounter. He approached the double mahogany wood doors and placed his key in the lock. He entered the stylish well furnished home. All he could smell throughout the house was the scent of vanilla and cinnamon. Then he laid eyes on her and it was all worth it.

Their eyes met in the dimly lit living room. Shades of Chocolate brown and burgundy filled the room. The flicker of vanilla candles gave the room a subtle glow.

There she lay on an oversized love seat draped in a sheer one-piece thong

Outfit and jeweled heals that exposed her entire foot. Next to the Love seat was a tray with various toppings, strawberries, chocolate syrup, vanilla syrup cool whip and her favorite frozen peaches. No words were exchanged she stood up and guided Noah toward the chair that she had prepared in the center of the room. She took his tongue in her mouth and played with it with just enough pressure. Noah moaned just from her touch. Then she slid down to her knees and opened his pants with her teeth to unleash his python. She undressed him nice and slow as he rubbed and pulled on her perky nipples.

Once she had him in full glory she poured chocolate syrup on his pleasure rod as she inhaled every inch of him. Noah squirmed in the chair and moaned as though he was a wounded animal. One treat after another adorned his shaft and each treat she put on she completely cleaned off. Noah's body began to shake and she knew what that meant. He wasn't ready for the party to end. Noah gathered enough breath to say "Shawty let me taste you" He picked her up and faced her head toward the top of the loveseat, he grabbed a frozen peach slice and began to insert it into her opening. He pushed in and out as she screamed in ecstasy. He held the peach slice on her clit and moved it slowly. The coldness from the ice sent chills up her spine she yelled "oh shit I cumin" one after another he pulled out of her.

When she had no more energy to cum again. He laid her side-ways spread her legs far apart and mounted her. His rod slid in with precision "emmmmmm" she whispered as he hit each spot inside of her. She rotated her hips in a snake like motion as he watched her beautiful round ass jump with each stroke. She proclaimed in her sexiest voice ever spoken, "Daddy I love how you feel inside of me" and before she could say anything else they both were singing in unison

"Oh, Oh, Oh TIFFFFFFFFFF!!!!!! Dis Pussy is so wet!" In a fit of orgasms Noah fell on top of Tiff and Tiff's body shook uncontrollably no other words were spoken. They both fell asleep comfortable in each other's love juices.

Across town Corn was preparing things for G's welcome home. He made sure he had enough cash lined up to get G a nice wardrobe and a fly whip, compliments of all the homies chipping in some stacks.

G was always a part of the squad and he put in plenty of work before getting booked for a petty ass drug charge that got him sent up for some years. Corn called G to be sure he was ready to go. "What up my nig"

Corn yelled through the phone, "Hello who's this"

"I'm sorry Mrs. Reynolds I was calling to speak with G is he there?" Corn felt stupid addressing G's mother like that. He whispered to himself "Dis nigga need a phone too, this shit got to stop." G made it to the phone gasping for air.

"Yo, Corn where you at?"

"I'm outside man come on we got stuff to handle, you got me talking all crazy to your mom hurry up man!"

"I'm on my way out, one."

G stepped outside and canvassed the block for Corn. He spotted him in a canary yellow Spider at the top of the block. His eyes grew with excitement as he approached the vehicle. He hopped in and as usual they greeted with a handshake and kept it moving. Corn and G said nothing as they blazed up the highway headed for a balers dream King of Prussia Mall. G adjusted his seat for comfort and they both nodded their head to classic Biggie Smalls "Life after Death" all the way to their destination. As they pulled up in the parking lot all eye were on them, even the sophisticated stuck up women stopped in their tracks. They wanted to see who was going to step out of one of the most expensive cars on the streets. Corn whipped into a free parking space and at the flick of a switch both butterfly doors flew open. He stepped out wearing a honey, crushed linen two piece pants set and camel skin loafers that played well off of his golden skin. The men approached the massive chrome double doors at the mall entrance and proceeded to glide in. G was no slouch either. He wore a fitted black tee with dark denim Red Monkey Jeans and some black on red throw-back #3 Jordans. He was equipped with that fresh prison glow and body that looked as if he was chiseled by an artist, 240lbs of all man. First stop was Louis Vutton store. G and Corn equipped themselves with watches, shoes and other fly accessories. Next stop was Bloomingdales this is where they purchased G's everyday wear, Denim, designer underwear and polo shirts. G was definitely happy to be home and happier that he had niggas that were real in the game. Corn and G laughed as they exchanged stories about TE` and their smuttin episodes. Corn stopped in the center of the mall to take a phone call. While he was on the phone G spotted a new store that looked like he could get some hot shit out of. He waved at Corn to get his attention.

"Yo, Corn." Corn approached G as he hung his phone up." What up dude?"

"You see that hot shit in the window what store is that?"

"Oh shit I almost skipped that one, That's Gees 2 Gents, I get all my exclusive shit from their let's go check it out" The two men entered the store and G went wild buying all that he could. As the two men were in the corner picking out custom shirts and hats they realized that they were under surveillance. Corn looked up and their eyes met. Cindy stood 5ft 5 and was half- black and Korean. She had hair that resembled 100% silk and two full breasts the color coffee and cream, which set up outside of her black suit jacket. Corn could do nothing but smile. "Damn I forgot she worked this shift" corn remarked to G who was still looking down at the shirts. G looked up just in time "Damn who dat?"

Corn replied, "That's Cindy, but I call her Candy because her ass is sweet like sugar."

"Do candy got a sister name cake? Cause a nigga definitely tryna bake something tonight" Corn gave him dap and crack a half smile. Cindy whispered in her co-worker's ear and gestured for corn to come over to the counter. Before G could finish talking, Corn had disappeared. Cindy escorted Corn to the back of the store without saying a word. Once in the back it was as if they were both animals. Cindy slammed Corn against the wall where racks of designer clothes hung. He reached up to grab hold of the shelf above him to brace himself for what was ahead of him. Cindy stood before corn now her black Armani suit was crumbled at her feet. And she wore nothing but black lace thongs with the diamond string a black lace push up bra and 3 inch black Kenneth Cole stilettos. She began to pleasure herself as Corn just stood there looking in amazement at how beautiful her body was. He thought to himself "Flawless." She slid Corn's pants down to his ankles and his boxer briefs went with them. Cindy squatted low to the floor with her legs spread wide and played with her clit slow and hard. She moaned and shook each time her soft fingers stroked up and she pulled on her ring that hung from her clitoris. Corn's rod was hard as cement. He began to stroke it and rub it gently on her lips. Cindy parted her lips and his rock hard extension filled every inch of her mouth. She moved her soft pink tongue round and round on the tip as she sucked with such force it echoed of the small storage room walls. Her body tremble and she made sensual hissing sounds with a mouth full of flesh. Corn pounded her face like he was in the pussy. She took every inch of him as it tickled the back of her throat. Cindy rode her own finger and slurped on Corn harder and harder. She could feel her nipples getting so hard that they tingled without any touch. She tugged at her clit ring and brought herself to climax. Her juices ran down both legs. Cindy's jaws tightened up as she came back to back. This was a chain reaction; Corn's body gyrated like he was a wild horse bucking. In one swift AWWWW he roared and his soldiers marched down Cindy's throat. Corn wiped his stick off and pulled up his trousers. Cindy smiled and whispered "call me later so we can finish what we stared." She then disappeared into the employee's only bathroom. Corn emerged from the back and was greeted by a smiling G with more bags than they could carry. "Corn smiled back and said "Now let's get your ass a blackberry for all the numbers you gone get at your party" Corn and G disappeared in the malls atmosphere.

A NOTE FROM THE AUTHOR

To all of my readers………

I thank you for all the support that you've shown me through this journey of mine. I am blessed by GOD to have such loyal readers that show genuine love. I am inspired by you all and hope that you will continue to take brief journeys away from reality with me. Continue to support and I will continue to write to my hearts' desires….

Love,

L J

INSIDE OUT 360
COMING FALL 2010

Evea's world gets turned INSIDE OUT as the ugly truth comes full circle!

PREVIEW TO MIND BODY & SOUL

(poetry for a life time)

Prisoner of Love

You got me!
My soul cries out to you,
Begging you to free me
I want to be free!
Free to love you and only you
I want to love you all day as we sit hand in hand,
Staring into each other's hearts
You control me
My every thought is of you
I dream sweet dreams of you
You hold me captive even in my slumber
My body is yours
Without a single touch it obeys your command
Your thoughts send gushing rivers between my Thighs
I'm yours
your prisoner of love
No shackles needed
Our love connection runs deeper than physical restraints
Our hearts speak the same language
We won't be satisfied with any other
I am your prisoner of love
Take me as I am
Love me as you will……

www.ingramcontent.com/pod-product-compliance
Lightning Source LLC
Chambersburg PA
CBHW030450250626
47154CB00003BA/1199

* 9 7 8 0 6 1 5 5 7 6 4 3 5 *